Eager and the mermaid

Also by Helen Fox

Eager

Eager's Nephew

Other books published by Hodder Children's Books

Otto and the Flying Twins

Otto and the Bird Charmers

Otto in the Time of the Warrior

Charlotte Haptie

Airborn

Skybreaker

Kenneth Oppel

There's More to Life

Far Out!

Rachel Billington

Eager and the mermaid

helen fox

A division of Hachette Children's Book

First published in Great Britain in 2007
by Hodder Children's Books

2

A Catalogue record for this book is available from the British Library

ISBN-13: 978 0 340 90256 1

Typeset in Perpetua by Avon DataSet Ltd,
Bidford on Avon, Warwickshire

Printed and bound in Great Britain by
Clays Ltd, St Ives plc

The paper and board used in this paperback by Hodder Children's Books are
natural recyclable products made from wood grown in sustainable forests.
The manufacturing processes conform to the environmental regulations
of the country of origin.

Hodder Children's Books
a division of Hachette Children's Books
338 Euston Road, London NW1 3BH
An Hachette Livre UK company

For Philip, the best of brothers, with love and gratitude

My thanks also to Nellie McElvey, Richard Webb and,
as ever, John Fox.

prologue

The governor sat in his office, reading his lexiscreen. A message scrolled across the top: *Any reports of strange finds or occurrences at sea are immediately to be investigated*. He sighed. As if he didn't have enough to do . . .

'Excuse me, sir.' Tanya, his animat-translator, put her head around the door. She had cool blue eyes and was programmed to speak sixty languages; but she had an annoying habit of twisting her blonde hair as she talked. Perhaps the manufacturers thought it made her more human.

She did it now.

'What is it?' he snapped.

'You're wanted on the beach,' said Tanya. 'Some fishermen have caught something.'

He raised an eyebrow. 'That's what fishermen do.'

Her blue eyes went blank. She repeated what she had said.

'What do the fishermen want – applause?' said the governor. 'I'm a representative of the Council of World

Governments. I'm not here to count fish.' Nonetheless, he stood up to go.

Outside was a din from the construction works. It hadn't rained for two years and the government was building a desalination plant. It would remove the salt from seawater and pump the fresh water all over the country.

He walked to the seashore through blistering heat. Nanofibres running through his pale suit kept his temperature down. The fishermen on the beach wore shorts and vests. About twenty of them stood there arguing.

'What are they saying, Tanya?' asked the governor.

An older man stepped forward. Tanya translated. 'You must speak to my sons.'

The fishermen fell silent and pushed a young man from their ranks. He was holding a cloth to his eye.

'Where's this catch of yours?' asked the governor.

'It punched me,' said the young man.

Tanya kept translating, twiddling her hair.

Another fisherman ran forward. 'My brother was struck by a fish's tail.'

The young man said angrily, 'I've been slapped in the face by a wet fish before. I tell you, it *punched* me!'

'Where is this fish?' demanded the governor.

The brothers looked at him in surprise. 'We let it go.'

The governor began to feel hot, in spite of his nanofibres.

'My nephews went to chase it,' said the father of the two men, pointing out to sea.

A fishing boat was bobbing on the shoreline. Two men jumped out and began pulling the vessel on to the sand. They shouted excitedly and beckoned their friends to help. The governor found himself running. He waded into the water, stumbling as he reached for the boat, peering inside. A net, scores of silver fish, seaweed, a slender arm . . .

Tanya was still on the beach. The governor bellowed to her: 'Call the military! I want this beach cordoned off.' He turned to the fishermen who were holding the boat steady. 'You caught a porpoise.' He could see they understood, and their eyes denied it. He said firmly, 'It was confused by the noise from the desalination plant.'

They looked at him, anger mingling with fear.

He steadied his breathing. 'Listen, I'm as confused as you are. But for all our sakes, keep quiet.'

one

All day, snow was falling. By the evening, a thick white carpet covered most of the countryside. A man trudging across the hilly fields was hard to spot. His raincoat, his boots, and even his hair camouflaged him against the snow.

The fields dropped steeply to a wood. When he was in line with a large oak tree, the white-haired man slithered down the slope. He pressed a device in his pocket and a crack appeared in the hillside, dislodging the snow. He was just able to squeeze through the gap. Stamping the snow off his boots, he went through a dark tunnel to a brightly lit room.

A robot stood waiting. She had a metal torso, and her arms and legs looked like a series of rubber rings. Her neat, oval head was rubber too. 'Hello, Professor,' she said. 'The sensor saw you. We weren't expecting you.'

'Hello, Allegra,' said the man, warmly.

A second robot entered. He was nearly identical to the first, but a little taller and his head was round.

'Professor Ogden!' he cried.

'Hello, Eager.' The professor took off his raincoat and shook the snow from it. 'Good disguise, eh? I must have looked like a walking snowman! That would have shocked anyone who saw me.'

Eager laughed. During his years with the Bell family, he and the children had built several snowpeople. Allegra showed no reaction. Although she was Eager's sister robot, she had never played with humans and never seen a snowman.

Professor Ogden hung up the raincoat.

'This garment is wet,' said the coat-hook. 'Shall I dry it for you?'

'Yes,' said the professor.

'Do you have news of the Bells?' asked Eager. It was customary for Professor Ogden to bring messages from the family.

The professor sat down on the only chair. 'I'm afraid I didn't have time to visit them. I've suddenly decided to go away. But you may be able to see them yourself shortly.' He leant back, as if waiting for the robot's reaction.

Eager tilted his head to increase the thinking power to his brain. It was too soon for his annual visit to the Bells. Did the professor mean the Ban would be over soon? The Ban was a law that forbade anyone from building self-aware robots. Even discussing the subject could land a scientist in prison. It was because of this law that the robots were in hiding.

'As you know,' said the professor, 'I spent last year travelling the world to persuade governments to end the Ban. I've reason to believe that the time has come. The announcement will be made in a few hours.'

A golden streamer flew across the room. 'We're free! We're free!'

Only the other robots could hear its high-pitched voice. The streamer became a ball of thousands of minuscule fibres and bounced in front of the professor.

'Jonquil – hello!' said Professor Ogden.

'Must we leave here?' asked Allegra.

'Dear Allegra, you don't mind the Ban, do you? You like being in hiding,' said the professor.

'I'm not in hiding,' she retorted. 'I've never lived in the human world and I don't want to. This is my home.'

'And I see no reason why you shouldn't stay,' said Professor Ogden. 'I can continue to visit you. I still need you and Jonquil to help me.'

'What should I do?' asked Eager.

'It's up to you,' said the professor. 'I created you, but you don't belong to me, any more than children belong to their parents. You can think for yourself and feel emotions, so you must be allowed to choose for yourself.'

Eager reflected. 'I'm a free agent.'

Professor Ogden said laughingly, 'Indeed. And when the Ban is lifted, you will be a *free* free agent!'

Eager laughed too, but uncertainly. He had waited years for the Ban to end, only to find that he was unprepared. 'I think . . . I would like to visit the Bells.'

The professor nodded. 'I'll arrange a delivery pod to take you.'

'No thank you,' said Eager hastily. 'I will make my own way there – I'm curious to see the world again.'

'Good for you,' said the professor.

Eager felt less sure of himself. It was a long time since he had been on his own in the world. Surely the professor would give him some advice? He was about to ask when the man said, 'I'm going away today. No one will be able to contact me.'

'Are you ill, Professor?' asked Allegra.

'No.' He smiled faintly. 'Though I am growing old, remember. I won't always be with you. But right now I need to disappear for a while.'

'Because of the Ban?' said Eager.

'Yes. We don't want people at my door looking for you the moment the Ban ends. So my laboratory is closed for the time being. I've encouraged my staff to have an extra holiday. When the fuss has died down, you and I can make contact.'

Jonquil became a streamer again, wrapping himself around Allegra's neck.

'Tell the professor about our work, Mother! We've built the fault-finding robots. They can't move and talk and think like us, but they can enter machines and repair them instantly, just like me.'

Allegra relayed what her son had said.

'Well done! I've always said how important this work is. And now, more than ever! But the world isn't ready. I must think carefully how to introduce these robots . . .' The professor's voice tailed off and he stared at the floor.

When he looked up again, his eyes were twinkling. 'You know my fondness for myths, Eager. I'm thinking now of the story of Prometheus.'

There was a pause. Eager waited to hear the story, but the professor was putting on his dry raincoat. 'This is the only help I can offer you now: whatever happens, Eager, be the very best you can. Be slow to give your trust, even when others say the right things.' He turned towards the tunnel as he spoke.

'Not trust people! That sounds frightening,' said Eager.

The professor faced him. 'There will be those you can trust, I'm sure. But you must be very careful. Listen to your conscience.'

'My conscience?' Eager exclaimed. 'Do I have one?'

Professor Ogden shrugged. 'You're conscious, aren't you? At least, you appear to be. That's why you've been hidden away all these years.'

'Yes . . .' said Eager uncertainly.

'Conscious and conscience. It's no coincidence that they sound alike.' Before Eager could ask more, the professor said, 'I must hurry. Goodbye, Eager. Goodbye, Allegra. Goodbye, Jonquil – be good.' He disappeared into the tunnel.

Outside, he bent down and scooped up handfuls of snow, patting them against the slope to disguise the secret doorway again.

two

At midnight, the robots gathered round a gobetween screen that showed a large building. Colourful national flags fluttered on the roof. A group of people stood on the terrace, as if posing for a holograph. In the middle of them was a friendly-faced woman in a yellow suit.

'What's happening?' asked Jonquil, perched as a triangle on Eager's shoulder.

'Nothing yet,' said his uncle. 'This must be the headquarters of the Council of World Governments. One of those people is the President.'

Silently, the people at her side stood back and the woman began to speak. 'This is the era of the robot,' she declared. The camera zoomed in until her face filled the screen and she seemed to be talking directly to the watching robots.

'Intelligent machines are our servants, freeing us to lead comfortable, fulfilling lives. They run our homes, offices, factories and transport.' Her tone changed. 'But the way has not always been easy. Many years ago, the most human-like robots the world had ever seen caused fear and alarm. They began to behave unpredictably, to do what *they* wanted, rather than what we wanted . . .'

Eager realized the President was talking about the BDC4 robots. He remembered those he had met and how they had destroyed themselves.

'The crisis was overcome,' said the President. 'But people questioned the wisdom of making robots that could think for themselves. Had we gone too far? It wasn't easy to answer this. No one wants to stop scientific progress, but your safety was at stake. After years of debate, the governments of the world came to a decision. We banned anyone from building self-aware robots. By self-aware, we mean able to reflect on their behaviour, and to feel emotions.'

'That's us!' cried Jonquil, becoming a star that twirled around the room.

The President paused for effect. 'This law – the Ban, as people call it – is now repealed . . .'

Jonquil stopped midair. 'Repeeled? How can you peel a law?'

'I think it means cancelled,' said Eager.

'Professor Ogden was right! We're free!' Jonquil jumped so high he brushed against the ceiling. He turned vivid red, extending and contracting the points of the star. 'Free! Uncle Eager can go back to the Bell family!'

'It depends what you mean by free,' said Allegra. 'Are we free to do what we want?'

'Listen,' said Eager. The President was still talking.

'Meanwhile, the governments of the world have conducted their own research. We conclude that self-aware robots are an impossibility. There is nothing to fear . . .'

Eager and his sister looked at each other, puzzled.

'However, it appears that before the Ban, some highly advanced – but not self-aware – robots were built. Their number and whereabouts are unknown. We hereby declare that no action will be taken against these robots or their owners,' said the President.

Jonquil bounced as a ball in front of his mother and uncle. 'What's the matter? Aren't you happy that the Ban is over?'

'Of course I am,' said Eager. 'I have been hiding for a long time.'

'Why did the President say robots like us are impossible?' asked Allegra.

'Let's go and see her, to show we exist!' cried Jonquil.

'I don't think the human world is as simple as that,' said Eager. 'If it was, Professor Ogden would have taken us to meet her before, to show we are not harmful.'

Jonquil sagged in the middle. 'Humans are very strange,' he said.

'It's night. We must turn down our power and process our thoughts,' said Allegra.

'What about the snow?' asked Jonquil.

'Too cold for you to go outside,' said his mother firmly.

'I didn't mean that. I mean, we didn't ask the professor about the snow,' said Jonquil.

'We were too busy hearing his news,' said Eager. His nephew was right. They should have asked the professor for an explanation. In all his years in the humans' world, it had never before snowed in the middle of summer.

three

Eager had his own room in the underground compound. Hidden cameras projected the view outside on to a gobetween screen. This was Eager's window on the world. After the announcement, instead of turning down his power, he stood and stared at the woods.

He knew snow to be very white, until people and vehicles left their muddy tracks behind. But under the moonlight the snow-capped trees were silvery. With a layer of snow over their summer leaves, they looked puffed-up. Eager was reminded of children in padded coats, quietly waiting to go out.

Eager was waiting too, but impatiently. When would the snow clear? And how would he get to the Bells' house?

He remembered the first time he made the journey. He had never before left the small room at the top of Professor Ogden's house, where he started life. The professor had built him to be as human-like as possible, and he was going out into the world to learn from his experiences.

Neither he nor the Bells knew what to expect. But he stayed with the family for many years, learning from the older children, Fleur and Gavin, and looking after Charlotte, the baby.

He glanced at a holograph of the family on the wall. It had been taken at Fleur's wedding to Sam. The bride and groom stood in the centre.

Eager had taken the picture. In those days, it was common to have a domestic robot, and people thought he was at the wedding to look after Charlotte, who was then a young girl. No one imagined he was a guest in his own right. It had been a happy day. Not long afterwards, the Ban began.

Eager had gone into hiding. Time stood still for him, until each summer, when he visited the Bells in secret and caught up with their news. He recalled memories of his visits . . .

A thought struck him. All the Bell children had grown up and left home. Gavin was an engineer, Fleur had a daughter of her own, and Charlotte was training to be a doctor. Would Mr and Mrs Bell want him back?

A movement in the holograph caught his attention. Every so often, the Bells relaxed their pose, turned to each other and smiled. Now they looked outward again and smiled, as if at Eager. He couldn't help smiling back. His anxiety lifted. Somehow he would get to the Bells' house, and see the family again.

He sat down and lowered his power. When dawn came, he felt refreshed. A paper-like sheet slipped under the door. It stood up and tottered on two corners towards him.

'It's warming up, Uncle Eager. Let's go and see the snow before it melts!'

four

Jonquil flew ahead and burst into a riot of colours – orange, yellow, pink, green, purple – as if to cheer up the monochrome world around him. Eager smiled to himself. For Jonquil, the wood was a giant playground. Sometimes Eager preferred to walk on his own, when he could feel the presence of the trees in peace.

He walked in the wood every day. No two visits were the same. Wind, rain and sunlight created a kaleidoscopic world. But however much the colours and shapes shifted, Eager could always find his bearings. Now the familiar landmarks – a gnarled oak here, a clump of pines over there – were all pale silhouettes under a parchment sky. The path, which yesterday twisted darkly through the wood, had disappeared.

Eager turned in the direction of the stream, or so he hoped. Each step was an effort, and he felt the cold of the snow. A snuffling beside him startled him. In full daylight, stood a badger.

Eager often met animals in the wood, though rarely nocturnal ones. If he made a rapid movement, they would run off. But if he stood still, they showed no fear of him. He guessed it was because he had no scent, unlike humans and other animals. Sometimes he had a sense that they were communicating with him, rather as Jonquil could send him thought-messages.

'Hello, Badger,' he said. 'This snow is very strange, isn't it?' He wished he could say something encouraging, but the weather forecast was more snow.

The badger shook its head. Eager thought that it was warning him about something.

'The food is still there,' he said, guessing that this was the source of the badger's anxiety. 'I'll ask the gobetween what badgers eat, then I'll come back and help find food for you.'

The animal gave him a final stare, as if it had more to convey. Then it ploughed its way through the snow into the undergrowth. Eager walked on until he recognized the ring of pines where the land began to slope again. Beyond was the stream. If it had frozen overnight, it might be starting to melt in the warmer temperature.

He reached the channel that the stream had made. The mossy stones were covered in snow. But there was no sign of water, or even ice.

The robot came every day to the stream. Depending on the weather, it was a gentle brook or a gushing torrent. One very hot summer it was nothing but a trickle. But it was always there.

He felt sad, and recognized a sense of loss. The stream is like me, he thought. From its source in the hills, the water went underground, emerging now and then into the daylight. Eager, too, was hidden in the hillside, coming out only for his daily walk or his secret visits to the Bell family.

Now Eager was free to come and go as he pleased; but the stream had disappeared.

As he climbed up the bank, he heard Jonquil's voice in his mind: 'There are humans in the wood.' He realized that this was what the badger had been saying!

In the clearing ahead of him, a man was crouched down. Eager stepped behind a trunk and peered out. He saw that the man was cradling a fawn, whose back legs were trapped in the snow. With his free hand, the man was scooping out a hole.

Although the animal didn't struggle, Eager's acute eyesight could tell that it was trembling. At last, it was able to stand. The man let go, and the young deer bounded away.

A woman, in the same green uniform as the man, came through the trees opposite Eager. He shrank back. She spoke, and the robot caught the words 'trail' and 'feed'. He guessed that their large backpacks contained food.

When they had moved away, he set off cautiously. It reassured him that people could be so kind to the forest animals. Surely they would help a robot too?

five

Ju woke up later than usual. She lay in her bed behind a screen in the living-room, gathering her thoughts. Her parents had woken her at midnight to say that the Ban was over and it was snowing. She had fallen straight back to sleep. Perhaps it had all been a dream.

Quickly, she pulled on the silky robe that was a present from her dad. She emerged from behind the screen and her jaw dropped. The terrace outside, with its table and chairs and tubs of flowers, had disappeared in a swirling snowstorm.

What if she was still dreaming? She thought of pinching herself. She had learnt in Biology that dreamers could still feel pain, but usually less so.

'Ow!' The pinch hurt a lot. Most likely, she was awake. So the ban was really over!

Ju remembered that snow had been forecast, although she had laughed at the idea. She walked down the hall to the kitchen. Fleur and Sam, her parents, sat at the table. They were still in their nightclothes. She noticed they looked bleary-eyed, as if they hadn't slept.

'It's snowing. In summer,' Ju declared. 'It *is* still summer, isn't it?' she added, in case she had been asleep for six months, like a character in a fairy tale.

'It *is* still summer,' agreed her mum. She yawned.

'Haven't you been to bed?' asked Ju.

'We had a lot to talk about,' said her dad, pouring himself coffee.

'I hope it was about Eager,' said Ju. 'When he comes out of hiding, can he live here?'

Her dad's eyes lit up. 'That would be fascinating. But there's hardly room for the three of us, let alone a full-size robot.'

'Now you work with Professor Ogden, we might move to a bigger house. You said so,' said Ju.

'But it hasn't happened yet,' said Sam, grinning.

Ju chewed her lip. Until recently her dad had worked on the moon, overseeing the robot factory there. He resigned and the professor, an old friend of the family, offered him a job. He was now happier in his work than he had ever been, but he still wasn't making his fortune.

Ju's thoughts returned to the robot. 'So will Eager go back to Gran and Grandpa's house?'

'I expect so,' said her mother.

'We've something to tell you,' said her dad, sounding unusually solemn.

Ju blinked. More news, and she hadn't even had breakfast. She sat down opposite her parents. A glance passed between them and Ju feared the worst. For years her dad had worked far from home, in dead-end jobs, because he spoke out against the Ban. Now that the Ban was over, perhaps Professor Ogden wanted to send him abroad to do research, or even back into space.

'Is it your work?' she asked, anxiously. 'Will you have to go away again?'

A shadow passed over Sam's face. To her relief, he said, 'Not in the way you think. This is good news. Professor Ogden has closed the laboratory and suggested his staff take a holiday.'

'Holiday?' echoed Ju. 'But we've just been on holiday. The new term is about to start. I'll miss all my friends and get behind in my projects . . .'

'You can stay if you prefer,' said her mother. 'I'd like to go, though.'

'Why do you have to go away?' asked Ju.

'Because the Ban has ended,' said her dad. 'Professor Ogden is one of the world's top technocrats. He's known to be interested in self-aware robots, but for years no one could talk about such things. Now there may be queues outside his laboratory . . .'

'Doesn't the professor want to talk about his work?' asked Ju.

'Yes, but to other scientists,' Sam replied, 'not to news reporters covering the Ban. Besides, Eager needs to settle into his new life quietly.'

'So *you* need to go away, too, in case people ask you questions,' said Ju.

Sam nodded.

'How long for?' Ju asked.

'A week or two, I should think.'

'You don't know?'

'The Ban will be stale news by then,' said Fleur, brightly.

Sam exclaimed, 'Then perhaps we can get on with some real research! There's more to science than building animats. They may look human but they haven't got two brain cells to rub together between them . . .'

Ju giggled. This was a favourite theme of her dad's.

Fleur leant across the table. 'What would you like to do, Ju?'

Ju had made her decision, but in case she was about to miss the holiday of a lifetime she asked, 'Where are you going?'

'Scotland,' said her mother. 'I've always wanted to go there. It's where your grandfather was born.'

Ju chewed her lip as she thought. She was sure there would

be other opportunities to visit Scotland. 'I'd like to stay with Gran and Grandpa,' she said. 'Anyway, you and Dad deserve a holiday together.'

'I'll go and ask them,' said Fleur.

Ju took a bowl of cereal into the living-room. What should she pack – winter clothes or summer vests? The weather wasn't the only thing that was topsy-turvy, she thought. Her whole day had been turned upside down.

She considered making up a story on the gobetween. Storytelling was her favourite pastime. But real life was strange enough, she decided. She stood by the window, mesmerized by the falling snow.

'Show me the weather news, Gobey,' she called.

The screen on the wall came to life. But instead of a discussion about the snow, it showed a city square under a clear blue sky. Hundreds of people, with angry or anxious faces, had crowded into the square. Children ran among them, creating games for themselves. Ju knew they were waiting for water tankers. The scene was happening all over the world as droughts took hold. Every day brought fresh pictures of dried-up riverbeds and cracked soil.

When the news reporter announced that this was southern France, Ju gasped. She had been there the previous summer. It was only a train journey away.

Her mother came in. 'Gran and Grandpa are expecting you

today. They couldn't be more pleased. And before you ask, Eager hasn't arrived yet!'

Ju looked back at the terrace. 'What's wrong with the weather, Mum? Why is it snowing in summer, and why are there droughts in the rest of the world?'

'Who knows?' said her mother. 'It could be global warming.'

'I thought the new technology fixed that,' said Ju.

Fleur sighed. 'So did we. I suggest you pack flexi-clothes. The forecast says more snow, but after that, who knows?'

'You keep saying "who knows",' grumbled Ju. 'It's the twenty-first century. You'd think scientists could predict the weather by now.'

'I agree,' said Fleur. 'Now, please get dressed. I told Gran we'd be there for lunch.'

Ju had expected her mum to say more. She was a food technologist and knew a lot about science. Perhaps she was so looking forward to going away with Sam that she didn't want to think gloomy thoughts about the weather.

Ju went behind the partition. 'Gobey, music!' she called out. Soon, she was throwing things into a bag and singing along to her favourite band. She picked out flexi-clothes – trousers that could be shorts and long skirts that became dresses. Reaching under the bed, she pulled out the legwraps that turned her shoes into boots. There were so few things in her bag that she added her new jumper for good measure.

Suddenly the music stopped. A man's voice cried, 'Hello, everyone! We're interrupting the show with a special message. Do you have a robot in a million?'

Pulling on her clothes, Ju paid only half-attention. It was another robot competition – which robot could run faster, crack eggs faster or decorate a room in record time. The robots, which were mainly animats, always got confused and made a terrible mess. The shows had been funny at first, but now Ju and her friends were bored of them.

'Perhaps your robot can calculate incredible sums or predict the weather? Does it show an unusual understanding of your funny little ways . . .'

This was not the familiar talk. One leg in her trousers, Ju hopped over to the gobetween. The presenter, Rick Rhodes, was as smiley as ever, but his tone was unusually serious.

'If you think your robot is a genius, we'd like to meet him or her. Robot Einstein, this is your moment!'

Ju hopped back behind her screen. It was about time they changed the show's format.

six

Ju's grandparents, Mr and Mrs Bell, lived in Wynston Avenue. Normally, it was a quiet residential street, but today delivery pods droned overhead. They landed in the road, releasing a small army of animats and vacubots. Ju watched as they fanned out along the street to clear away the snow.

Fleur and Sam had walked ahead from the hoverbus stop and Ju took long strides to catch up with them.

'Someone's had a party,' said her dad, peering over a wall. A wizard's wand had been thrust into a white flowerbed, and a pair of silver shoes stood neatly on the doorstep.

'The wizard magicked the princess away,' said Ju.

'Oh no,' said Sam with a smile. 'She left by tele-transportation.'

Ju laughed. 'It'll never happen.'

'People said that about flying,' said her dad. 'Mark my words, we're on the edge of a scientific breakthrough. Understanding consciousness . . . The Ban held us up. But now there's nothing to stop us moving on. And moving matter around may be part of it!'

Ju was so struck by the idea of things vanishing and reappearing elsewhere, that she started to weave it into a story. She fell behind her parents again.

'Look at those animals going into people's gardens! I wouldn't let them in if you paid me!'

Startled, Ju searched for the speaker. A neighbour she didn't recognize was standing behind her hedge. Ju thought she must have misheard her. 'You mean *animats*?'

'Animals, I call them,' said the woman. 'I hired some cleaner-clones last month, after my husband's birthday party. They left my house in a worse state than when they started.'

Her grandmother wrote job descriptions for robots, so Ju knew something about their capabilities. She said helpfully, 'Perhaps you got the wrong animats. They were programmed to do a different job.'

'Create a pigsty, you mean?' the neighbour exclaimed. 'It costs enough to hire them, believe me.' She went indoors.

Ju felt sorry for the woman, but she couldn't help grinning as she wondered what the cleaner-clones had done. She ran after her parents. They had reached the bend in the road where the Bells' glass house stood. Ju's grandfather had designed it when he was a young architect. The vast lime tree in the front garden was yellow-white with blossom and snow. After the frost, the flowers would quickly fall, Ju thought sadly.

Mr and Mrs Bell welcomed them from the front step. As they entered, a green light by the door flickered. 'We're so pleased you're coming to stay, Ju,' said a silky feminine voice. 'We've prepared your mother's old room.'

'Thank you, house,' said Mrs Bell. 'I couldn't have put it better myself.'

Fleur rolled her eyes. 'This house is becoming too big for its boots. You talk to it too much, Mum.'

'Well, working at home is very lonely,' said Mrs Bell.

'Is Eager here?' asked Ju, peering down the hallway as if the robot might be hiding there.

'Not yet,' said her grandmother.

Mr Bell said gently, 'Chloe, we can't be sure he's coming.'

'You're right, Peter, we can't be sure.' Mrs Bell winked at Ju. 'Though I still expect him. This is his home, after all.'

After lunch, Ju waved goodbye to her parents. They were catching the hovertrain to Scotland that evening.

Mrs Bell gave Ju a hug. 'It's a lovely surprise for us to have you here. And we have a surprise for you too.'

Ju took a sharp intake of breath. Surprises were hardly short on the ground that day, though she didn't like to say so. The weather had gone haywire, the Ban had ended, and her parents had left unexpectedly.

'What is it, Gran?' she asked, as brightly as she could.

'Finbar is coming to stay, too.'

Ju was lost for words. Fortunately, her grandmother had more to say. 'Marcia is flying in for a major exhibition of her work . . .'

Ju nodded. Marcia Morris, her mother's best friend from childhood, was a well-known artist. All over the city, there were billscreens advertising the exhibition.

'But it seems she still has work to do. She'll be shut away in a studio, and poor Finbar will be left on his own in the hotel,' said Mrs Bell. 'When we heard, we invited him to stay here. We weren't expecting you to come. But you became good friends last year, didn't you?'

Ju nodded. It was true. She had met Marcia's son the previous summer and they had kept in touch on the gobetween. But for a whole month Finbar hadn't returned her calls.

'You'll be company for each other,' Mrs Bell went on.

With a jolt, Ju realized that her grandmother had taken her silence for agreement. Of course, she could hardly say otherwise. She swallowed. 'When is Finbar coming?'

'Tomorrow,' said Mrs Bell.

seven

Finbar lay on his back, an arm over his eyes shielding them from the sun. There were voices in the background as people said goodbye. He was sorry it was time to leave. After a month, the house on the mountain had come to feel like home.

Spreading his fingers, he peeped at the sky. As usual, it was blue and endless. There had been no clouds overhead for the entire month. Without rainfall, water had become in short supply, and for the last week it had been rationed.

To leave before the rains came felt like abandoning a story halfway through, just as suspense was building.

But it's time to go, Finbar thought. My own life must move on. There were places to visit, things to learn, friends and family to see again. He had been due to spend the next month with his mother. But Marcia was busy preparing for an exhibition of her paintings, so he was going to stay with her old friends, Mr and Mrs Bell.

He liked the Bells very much, and their granddaughter,

Ju, had become a good friend. Well, it wouldn't be long. A few hours by Sorbjet the next day, and he would be with them . . .

Finbar let his thoughts drift away, as he had learnt to do during his stay. An eagle hovered above him. For an instant, Finbar felt that he was the bird, looking down on himself. It was a perfect moment. No hopes or worries interfered with it. Just the thought: I am the bird; the bird is me.

He was suddenly aware of discomfort. Small stones were digging into his bare arms. He sat up and rubbed the crisscross marks they had left. An insect had bitten his ankle. He yawned.

'Finbar!'

'Coming, Dad.'

Brushing the dust from his shorts, he strolled towards the house. The sun was high now and he had to squint to see the man on the front steps. Amir was carrying a bag across his shoulder. He stepped down to meet his son.

He said, 'It's a bit late to ask, Finbar, but I hope you've been taking your sunscreen pills.'

'Mostly.' Finbar grinned. His tan made him almost as dark as his father. It was typical that Amir had only just noticed. He was a poet, and often seemed to be in a world of his own.

Amir looked relieved. 'Good. I should hate to face Marcia otherwise. Your mum made me promise . . . oh! Several things. I've forgotten them, as usual.'

'Don't worry,' said Finbar. 'She'll see that I'm well. I'm so healthy I must be glowing.'

'Well, we need to get moving if we're going to meet her in time,' said Amir. He held out his hand, palm uppermost. 'I fetched this from the office for you.'

It was Finbar's jinn. He remembered how odd it had felt to part with it. But that was weeks ago, when he arrived. Now it seemed odd to put it on again. He hesitated.

'I can guess how you feel,' said his dad. 'I wrote a poem about my jinn, called *Magic cell*:

'Featherlight, my handcuff weighs me down
Liberator, it binds me to you.'

Finbar slipped the jinn on to his wrist. It irritated him, but he knew that he'd soon get used to it. Of course it wasn't magic, but it *was* strange, the pull it began to exert over him. Already he was thinking of the friends he would call.

'You don't want to stay here for ever, do you?' said his dad.

Finbar shook his head. 'I can come back though?'

'Any time you like. With or without me.' Amir draped an arm across his son's shoulder. 'We've said goodbye, so let's go.'

Finbar noticed his backpack resting against the wall. He hoisted it on and joined his dad on the path down the mountain.

They passed the terraces for growing vegetables. Finbar remembered with pride the backbreaking hours he had spent digging the irrigation channels. Now the rainfall that would have trickled away down the mountain would be directed to the crops – if it ever came.

The path narrowed and Finbar fell into step behind Amir. He called, 'Why has it stopped raining, Dad? Not just here, but all over the world?'

'It hasn't stopped raining as such,' said Amir. 'But the rain falls in the wrong place.'

Finbar smiled to himself. 'How can there be a wrong place for rain?'

Amir looked round at him. 'The sea?'

'I *see* what you mean, Dad. Sorry! Bad pun,' said Finbar. He fell silent, trying to figure out why rain should avoid the land, until he reminded himself that the best scientists in the world didn't know either.

They reached the village and sat outside the main café, waiting for a hovercar.

An animat-waiter brought them tea. Finbar had grown up with animats and took them for granted, but this was the first one he had seen in a month. He stared at him. It was an early model, the face and hair obviously artificial. The newer animats were far more convincing, and sometimes even Finbar had to double-check they were robots.

Finbar toyed with his jinn. There were several messages. Should he call someone now, or wait until he reached the city? He decided to do neither. He had gone without technology for weeks: he could wait a bit longer and see his friends in person.

An elderly man in a long robe approached. He greeted Finbar's father with a handshake, and gave him something. Finbar caught the glint of metal. Was it an ancient coin?

He waited until the man had walked on. 'Is that old money, Dad? Why did he give it to you? Is it lucky or something?'

Amir burst out laughing. He uncurled his hand, revealing a small silver disc. 'Last time I was here, a local singer set my poems to music. This is a recording of them.'

'Stupid me,' said Finbar. 'Cognitive failure.'

'I don't know about lucky,' said Amir, slipping the disc into his tunic pocket. 'But it *is* magic. And unlike magic in the past, we can understand how it works. We can all be magicians today.'

Finbar scuffed his sandals in the dust. Fancy not recognizing a disc! He said hesitantly, 'I suppose . . . when you haven't been around technology for a while, life starts to seem mysterious. You almost believe anything could happen, even without machines.'

His dad nodded. 'Why do you think I come here so often? Here's the hovercar.'

Finbar and his father climbed in. The hovercar rose a metre

from the ground and glided away from the village. Finbar craned his neck to look back at the mountain, hoping the rains would hurry up. He imagined water flowing down the irrigation channels, and the earth gratefully receiving it.

eight

Eager grew impatient to leave for the Bells' house. He could no longer concentrate on his daily routine of helping Allegra in her work and studying on the gobetween. He decided to set off, in spite of the snow. Allegra heard the news calmly. Jonquil was curled as a ball on a table in the laboratory. He was motionless and Eager guessed he was working within the gobetween.

'Jonquil's testing the latest fault-finding robots,' confirmed Allegra.

The fibres that made up Jonquil were covered in microscopic cilia, like the hairs on a leaf. These cilia could detach themselves and enter a machine to correct a fault or reprogram it. The fault-finder robots were even smaller than the cilia. Eager imagined them whizzing around inside the gobetween, exploring its molecular structure.

'I'm going to walk in the wood before I leave,' said Eager. 'I will say goodbye later.'

Earlier that morning, through the window, he had seen the

people in green uniforms leave food for the animals and then depart. Dogs and their walkers had come and gone too. It was safe to go out.

Eager lifted his feet carefully through the snow, hurrying as best he could to the stream. He had little hope that the water had returned, but he couldn't leave without knowing.

The channel was covered in snow. Small footprints went round and round in circles and crisscrossed on top of each other. Deer must have come looking for water.

As Eager peered into the hole from which the water normally gushed, there was an outburst of radiant light. He staggered backwards crying, 'Sphere?' He thought he had seen the shape of a ball. The light grew steady, and he saw that he was right.

At points in his life, the luminous ball had guided him. Months or years might pass until it appeared again, and Eager had learnt never to expect it. But he knew that when Sphere did come, something important was about to happen. It would convey to him a thought, or a feeling, that helped him.

'Sphere, what does it mean?' he said. 'Why has the stream dried up?'

The light grew less, like the dying rays of a sun. Eager had a sensation of dread. Was that what Sphere wanted him to feel? He stepped over the stones to firmer ground and told himself there was nothing to be afraid of.

Light radiated from the ball once more, as it floated towards a pine tree. Merging with the bark, it vanished. A bird, taking flight, beat the leaves of the neighbouring tree. Snow plopped to the ground.

Eager waited, though he knew from experience that Sphere was unlikely to reappear. He felt encouraged and guessed that was why Sphere had come.

Now, all he could think about was seeing the Bells again. He hurried back to the compound to say goodbye to the other robots.

nine

Ju woke up in her mother's old bedroom. She lay there, enjoying the luxury of a big bed and lots of space. The blinds opened and light poured in. She wondered how her parents were. They had called the previous night to say they had arrived in Scotland.

On the whole, life had been normal since her dad's return to Earth. But there was a cloud of mystery hanging over his time on the moon. He had been present when a strange signal came from outer space, and the International Space Authority secretly took him away to be debriefed.

Sam refused to discuss the signal, and there was no mention of it on the gobetween. It was as if the incident had never happened. With her fondness for storytelling, Ju had imagined all kinds of scenarios. Perhaps this year the truth would come out. Was an alien civilization trying to contact humans?

Impulsively, she went to the window and looked at the sky.

Perhaps the Listening Station on the far side of the moon was picking up another signal that very minute . . .

A flash in the garden below caught her eye. She blinked, thinking she had imagined it. There it was again! She pulled on her clothes and ran downstairs. Her grandparents were having breakfast in the kitchen. 'I'm just going outside!' she called.

A green light by the front door flickered. 'Where's your coat?' said a melodious voice.

'I'm wearing a jumper!' said Ju.

'You need a coat,' said the house. 'It's bitterly cold.'

Ju wondered how a machine could judge whether cold was bitter or not. She said, 'This is a wool jumper. It's very warm. My friend Luisa knitted it for me.'

The door stayed closed. Ju tried not to fume. Her dad always said it paid to explain things to machines.

She quickly recited, 'Wool has been scientifically proved to insulate as well as any of our modern materials. And sometimes better. Now will you open the door?'

'How interesting,' said the house. 'Wool comes from sheep, doesn't it?'

'Open the door!' yelled Ju.

The front door opened. 'There's no need to shout,' said the silky voice.

Ju hurried into the garden. The house was right: it was very cold. Snow lay everywhere, and the path was slippery with frost. No light was flashing at the bottom of the garden. She must have seen a reflection from the sun. Still, she was pleased to be outside. The stone bench by the wall had heat-wires that kept it clear of snow. She sat there, enjoying the contrast of chill air against her face and the snug warmth of her body.

Time passed as she juggled with ideas of stories in her head. Her attention wandered to a bush with bright yellow buds. It began to shine, so brightly that she turned away. When she looked back, a light was moving towards her. Ju gasped. It was like a miniature sun!

She gripped the edge of the bench. 'What are you?' she cried. She recalled the spybots she had seen in movies, but this was far stranger.

The rays subsided. Glowing gently, the ball hovered before her.

Ju felt calm again. She waited – what for, she didn't know.

The ball floated on. Reaching the fence, it passed through and disappeared.

'Ju! Ju! Are you all right?'

She stood up. Finbar was at the edge of the wild patch at the end of the garden, a small backpack at his feet. Her first thought was that he always travelled light. When they went to ISA's headquarters the previous summer he had taken an even tinier backpack.

'I've been calling you. You were staring into space,' said Finbar.

Ju said, 'I just saw something strange – a floating ball, like a sun. It went through that fence.'

'Through the fence?' said Finbar, following her gaze.

Ju nodded. 'It sounds weird, I know.'

'Passing through matter is a quantum effect,' said Finbar. 'No one can make it happen outside a laboratory.'

'I know,' said Ju. She added hotly, 'But I didn't imagine it.'

'Never said you did. Anyway, hello.' He grinned.

'Hello,' she said. She noticed that he had grown more than she had, and they were the same height now.

Finbar had been wondering how Ju might greet him, but he had not expected the coolness of her stare. He blurted out, 'Listen, I don't want to spoil your time with your grandparents. I don't have to stay here. Mum's living in her studio, but I can go to the hotel.'

'Don't be silly,' said Ju. 'You can't stay in a hotel on your own.'

'And Mum's arranged for me to go to your learning centre,' said Finbar. 'But I can change that.'

'I don't mind,' said Ju, staring at her feet.

'So why are you cross with me?' asked Finbar.

She took a moment to reply. 'Why didn't you answer my calls?'

'Didn't my jinn answer?' said Finbar. 'I left an automatic message.'

Ju's head shot up. 'That said you were meditating? I believed it the first time, but not after a month!'

Finbar groaned. 'The message was a short way of saying "I'm on a retreat with my dad".'

'How would I know that?' asked Ju. 'And what's a retreat?'

'My other friends understood, but I suppose you haven't known me long enough,' said Finbar.

Ju was not placated. 'You could have called me back.'

'No jinn, no gobey,' said Finbar, shrugging.

She took a moment to understand. 'You mean, you never heard my message? Even in outer space you can connect to the gobetween. Where *were* you?'

'Up a mountain,' said Finbar. 'There was no gobetween and my jinn was locked in the office. On the retreat, everyone agrees not to have outside communication.'

'So that's why it's called a retreat – you're retreating from your friends!' retorted Ju.

Finbar couldn't help laughing. 'It was only for a month. Anyway, I'm glad we're still friends.'

'I didn't say we weren't . . .' Ju broke off. 'Well, perhaps I did. Shall we sit on the bench? It's lovely and warm. How did you study without a gobey?'

'Books!' hissed Finbar, as if reminding her of a long-lost

artifact. 'And lots of the people there were experts. They taught me all sorts of subjects.'

'What else did you do?'

'Swam in the rock pool – it was really hot. And I went walking and climbing with Dad and some other boys.'

'So it was a holiday?' said Ju.

'I wouldn't say that.' Finbar showed her his calloused palms. 'I helped grow vegetables, and we dug an irrigation channel to water them. Only it wouldn't rain.'

Ju cried, 'It's happening everywhere!'

'I know,' said Finbar. 'The weather's all wrong.' He saw that her gaze was wandering. 'Are you waiting for that ball to come back?'

'Not waiting. I've no reason to expect it,' said Ju. 'But it was strange – I had the feeling it was saying something.'

'What?' asked Finbar.

'I've no idea.' Ju smiled at the absurdity.

'We'd better go inside,' said Finbar. 'Mum's there, with Gavin. I forgot – they've something to tell you.'

'Uncle Gavin?' said Ju.

'He met us at the airport.' As they walked towards the house, Finbar added, 'We can ask your grandparents about the light ball. Perhaps it's something they've installed in the garden.'

ten

Ju's grandparents were in the living-room with her uncle, Gavin, and Marcia. Gavin stood up and gave his niece a bear-hug. 'I thought you were going to Dublin to build a bridge,' said Ju.

To her surprise he turned pink. Her mum had told her that he often blushed as a boy, but Ju had never seen it happen till now. 'I'm leaving tomorrow,' said Gavin. 'I had something important to do first.'

Marcia hugged Ju too, enveloping her in perfume. 'It's lovely to see you again. Such a shame that Fleur and Sam are away.'

Ju didn't think it was a shame from her parents' point of view. She said, 'Professor Ogden closed his lab, so they took a holiday.' She noticed that her uncle had not sat down again. He was standing beside Marcia, smiling. They were both smiling.

'Would you like some cake, Finbar?' asked Mrs Bell.

Finbar was leaning against the wall. 'In a minute, please,' he said. 'I'm waiting for Mum and Gavin to get to the point.'

Gavin burst out laughing. Marcia looked bashful, which was something else Ju had never seen before. Marcia Morris was the most self-assured person she had ever met.

Her uncle cleared his throat. 'Well, there's a reason I haven't left for Dublin yet. Marcia and I have come to tell you we're getting married.'

'Oh,' said Mrs Bell, clamping a hand to her mouth.

'It's a bit sudden, I agree,' said Gavin. 'We've only known each other for twenty years.'

'I don't believe in rushing into things either,' said Mr Bell. 'But I'm glad you've decided.'

'Congratulations!' cried Mrs Bell, and for a moment everyone was kissing and hugging each other, including Ju and Finbar.

Marcia said in mock reproach, 'Gavin, you know perfectly well we hadn't seen each other for years – until last summer.' She added, 'Ever since, Gavin's been flying round the world to meet me while I was touring with my exhibitions.'

'We thought you were travelling for work, Gavin,' said Mrs Bell.

'I was,' said Gavin, blushing again. 'I just took a few detours.'

Ju was looking at Finbar, wondering what he was feeling.

'Could I have that cake now, Mrs Bell?' he asked, settling on a floor cushion.

'Of course,' said Ju's grandmother.

Gavin and Marcia sat down again.

'When are you planning to get married?' asked Mr Bell.

Marcia said matter-of-factly, 'The Saturday after next.'

Mr and Mrs Bell gasped in unison. Even Ju, who knew little about weddings, thought this was very soon.

'We're both so busy for the next few months that then's the only time we can take a honeymoon,' said Marcia.

'You might say we've waited long enough,' said Gavin. 'We'd get married tomorrow, but Marcia has to finish her paintings and I have to go to Dublin.'

'The wedding is just after my exhibition opens,' said Marcia. 'I hope I've got the paint out of my hair by then!'

Mrs Bell leant forward eagerly. 'What sort of wedding are you planning?'

'A quiet one,' said Marcia. 'Our families and a few close friends. Nothing elaborate.'

Ju gave a sigh of relief. She knew from the gobetween that bridesmaids were fashionable again. She had been silently praying that Marcia wouldn't ask her to be one.

Marcia was saying, 'We'll have a big party later in the year for the rest of our friends.'

Finbar muttered, 'Half the art world, a few famous actors, gobey-show hosts . . .'

Ju gave him a sympathetic look. She knew how much Finbar hated such parties. 'Shall we go outside again?' she whispered.

In the doorway, she remembered the glowing ball and turned back. Her grandmother was saying, 'Are you getting married in a house of faith?'

'Yes,' said Marcia. 'It's an unusual one . . .'

Ju joined Finbar in the hallway. She would ask her grandparents about the ball later.

'I want you to know,' a voice purred, 'how delighted I am to welcome you and Marcia into the family.'

Finbar stammered, 'Um . . . er . . . thanks, house. I'm very honoured.'

Ju could hardly contain herself as they walked to the back garden. 'Don't you mind?'

Finbar was busy pulling on his coat. 'Mind what?'

'Your mum getting married,' she said.

'Why should I mind?' said Finbar. 'I like Gavin a lot.'

'But you've been on a retreat. She couldn't contact you,' said Ju. 'She must have decided to get married without asking you.'

Finbar said, 'Actually she sent me a letter . . .'

'A letter?'

'A delivery pod brought it to the mountain. It must have cost a fortune,' said Finbar. 'But she didn't need to ask me. I'd already told her to marry Gavin if the opportunity arose. I made it sound like a joke.'

'*If the opportunity arose?*' mimicked Ju. 'Whatever gave you that idea?'

He sat down on the stone bench. 'Let's just say I had a hunch when I saw them together last summer. And Gavin seemed very keen to make friends with me.'

'No one else had a hunch,' said Ju. She took a deep breath. 'Will Gavin be your stepfather?'

'Of course,' said Finbar.

'Doesn't your dad mind?' asked Ju.

Finbar looked surprised. 'He'll always be my dad. Anyway, he wants Mum to be happy. Now he can move on in his own life. He might stay at the retreat.' He was astonished to hear himself say this. It sounded true, though his dad had never said so. Lately, he had begun to have flashes of knowing things.

Ju wondered whether family relationships were easier if you spent a lot of time up a mountain. She said, 'We'll be step-cousins, won't we?'

'You can drop the "step", if you like,' said Finbar.

Ju bit on her lip. 'I don't have any other cousins.'

'I've loads,' Finbar said, quickly adding, 'but they're all babies. It'll be good to have one my age.'

eleven

Inside the compound, Allegra presented Eager with a pair of slender white planks. 'Skis,' she explained. 'I've just made them for you, with the latest friction-reducing technology. They're voice-activated.'

Eager took them gratefully. The hills were still snowbound and it would be hard to progress on foot.

'I haven't had time to test them,' said Allegra.

Jonquil's enthusiasm made it easier to say goodbye. The golden ball zoomed around the room, calling, 'He's off to see the Bells!'

Eager remembered that on his last visit Jonquil had stowed away. He said, 'You can come too, Jonquil. You won't have to hide this time – the Bells know all about you.'

Jonquil stopped spinning. His thin treble voice said, 'I'd like to stay here, if you don't mind.'

'No,' said Eager. 'But don't you want to find out more about the world? And see the Bells again?'

'I liked the human world,' said Jonquil. 'It was exciting and new, and I liked your friends. But when I came home, I realized I belong with other robots. Humans have created their world for them, not me. I can operate their machines, but I can't handle their objects. And your friends can't hear me speak. You have to speak for me. I like the rest of the world too, the trees and plants and animals, but I don't belong there either.'

He became a spiral, twisting furiously as if to bore a hole in the floor. Springing up, he said, 'You see, Uncle Eager? I don't even fit in this house. It's built like a human's house, because that's how people build things, and you're human-shaped. But I don't have a body, or limbs. I don't need doorways or straight walls or tables.'

This was the longest speech Jonquil had ever made.

'Yes, I see,' said Eager. 'Even clever humans, such as Professor Ogden, don't understand what robots like you want. It's hard to imagine.'

Allegra said quietly, 'I'm glad you're staying, Jonquil.'

The robots said goodbye. Eager stepped on to his skis and out into the world.

First Eager skirted the wood. The skis sped smoothly over the snow. He felt so secure that he let his thoughts wander. He recalled the badger and was pleased that the humans would be feeding him. He wondered where Professor Ogden had gone and hoped he was taking a proper holiday.

He had forgotten to ask the gobetween to tell him about Prometheus, the myth that the professor had mentioned. Eager knew what a myth was. Gavin Bell had once explained to him that it was a very old story that might echo a half-known truth, but was made up like a fairy tale.

Gavin had given Eager some myths to read. He enjoyed them, but one thing puzzled him. How would he have known the stories were made up if Gavin hadn't told him? If he, a robot, could exist, couldn't young men be turned into trees, and creatures called gods live in the sky and sea?

Remembering this, Eager stared at a tall beech tree as he passed. Its branches reminded him of arms reaching for the sky. What was to say that it wasn't once a boy? Or that it might not become a boy in future? Of course, one of the first things Eager had learnt was that people and objects didn't change. People didn't become horses, or horses become cauliflowers.

Even so, he had discovered that much of the physical world should not be taken at face value. Water that flowed the next day might be solid – or disappear altogether, like the stream. The world was a strange place and however much he learnt about it, he was constantly surprised.

It was time to go up the hill to reach the main road. Eager expected a gentle climb, but the skis shot forward like rockets.

A tree popped up and he slalomed past it. He struck the side of a rock and for a moment was horizontal. His arms flapped as he found his balance.

'Whoa!' he cried, but the skis seemed not to understand. It was very different to his meander past the wood. The field dipped. He plunged down, sailing up the opposite bank. He hit a series of bumps, landing pigeon-toed each time. The skis righted themselves, hurtling him forward again.

He was thankful to see a fence ahead. The main road must be the other side. 'Slow down!' he called. The skis stopped so abruptly that he somersaulted over the fence, across the road, and into a snowdrift. A passing hovercar swerved to miss him.

'What on earth are you doing?' cried a voice.

Eager excavated himself from the snow and peered out. An angry-looking woman stood over him. 'How dare you catapault yourself into my path!'

Eager considered this. Strictly speaking, he had not catapaulted himself at all. But he *had* been operating the skis, so he must take some responsibility. He opened his mouth to explain.

'You robots are a menace,' said the woman.

Through the back windows of the hovercar, two pairs of awe-struck eyes looked out. Eager smiled and waved to show that he was friendly and not a threat.

'No point in waving at the children,' snapped the woman.

'They're travelling through the Amazonian jungle.'

Eager stared at the boy and girl. They must be watching a simulation. He tried to imagine a jungle, wondering what they could see instead of him through the green-tinted windows.

'What are you doing here?' said the woman. 'Where are your owners?'

Eager hesitated. 'I'm alone. I would like a ride to the city, please.'

The woman laughed. 'The city! Going there to make your fortune, are you?'

Eager laughed too, to be polite.

She glared at him. 'Why are you going to the city?'

'To meet friends.'

'Oh, don't tell me,' said the woman. 'You've a date at the theatre.'

'Not tonight,' said Eager. 'But I enjoy the theatre. Do you?'

'How dare you!' stormed the woman. 'You robots act as if you're clever, but you only mimic us!'

She climbed into the hovercar and pulled away with the door still open. It struck Eager, toppling him into the snowdrift again. He lay there, bewildered, as the hovercar sped away. The woman was furious. What had he said to annoy her?

As he pondered, a glint in the sky caught his attention. It must be a flying pod, though it made no hum. Eager watched for the flash of light to reappear. Slowly, down through the white sky, came a winged golden creature. A god, riding in his chariot! Eager told himself it was impossible. But what if the myths were true after all?

Could it be an angel? He had looked at pictures of angels, and he knew that some people claimed to have seen them, although no one could say with any authority what they really looked like.

By now the creature was floating between the treetops and Eager recognized it. It was a robot in a flying machine. A BDC4. An angel would have astonished him less.

twelve

The BDC4 robots had been built at the same time as Eager. Professor Ogden helped design them when he worked for LifeCorp. His colleagues secretly wanted to copy the brains of dead people into the robots. He argued that it was too dangerous and resigned from his job.

Eager had to learn things through experience and made lots of mistakes. The BDC4s understood the human world at once, which impressed everyone. But soon the pull of their previous memories was too much. They behaved strangely, setting out to do the things they had most enjoyed as humans.

Eager remembered all this as he waited for the flying machine to land. He saw that it was a curved seat under a glass semi-sphere. The stubby golden wings were attached to the sides.

The glass top opened and the pilot climbed out. It was definitely a BDC4. There was no mistaking the long, sculpted limbs and domed head. It hurried towards Eager.

'Allow me to help you.' The voice was deep and male. 'I saw that hovercar knock you over.'

Eager clasped the robot's strong hand and was hauled to his feet. The BDC4 was a good deal taller than he was. Close to, his gold was tarnished in places, and there were dents and scratches on his body. Of course, he was no longer new. He was nonetheless graceful and dazzling.

'Are you all right?' he asked.

Eager stared at the robot. Once, he had longed to make friends with a BDC4, but those he met were hostile. Now, a BDC4 was concerned about him!

He managed to say, 'I'm all right now, thank you. But I was shocked to be knocked over, and my system was shocked by the cold snow.'

'A shocking experience all round,' said the BDC4, solemnly. 'Did I see you talking to the driver of the hovercar?'

Eager nodded. 'I wanted a lift.'

'A hitchhiking robot!' cried the BDC4. 'And the driver knocked you over? Shocking!'

For some reason, Eager had an urge to laugh. 'Yes, it was shocking. I asked her politely.'

'Well, where are you going?' said the BDC4.

'To the city, the old professional quarter,' replied Eager.

'I know it. I'll take you!' The robot led the way to the flying machine. It was as high as his waist and the seat was narrow.

'Squeeze in,' he said. The robots wedged themselves side by side and the BDC4 pressed the control panel.

'I call it Orville, in honour of one of the pioneers of flight,' he said.

Orville began its soundless ascent. Soon it was level with the trees, following the road. Below, the snowy landscape stretched as far as Eager could see. The silence made him think, This is what it's like to be a bird, or a floating leaf.

Some minutes later he said, 'I beg your pardon. My name is Eager.'

'Cedric,' said the BDC4.

'Orville is a wonderful machine, Cedric. Did you build it?' asked Eager.

The robot took a moment to reply. 'My owner did. He hoped there would be more, but he died before it could go into production. It's the only one of its kind.'

'I'm sorry,' said Eager. 'About your owner, that is. It's very painful to lose someone, isn't it?'

The BDC4 glanced at him, too quickly for Eager to read his expression. 'Yes,' he said. 'It's painful.'

They sat in silence for a while. 'How is Orville powered?' asked Eager.

'Antigravity.'

Eager cried, 'Antigravity! Your owner must have been very clever.'

'He was.' Cedric looked down. They had reached a busy highway. 'Better go cross-country, I fancy. We don't want to be all over the gobey news tonight.' The flying machine swung to the right.

Eager certainly didn't want to be news on the gobetween, but he wondered about his companion. 'Don't you want everyone to admire your flying machine?'

Cedric gave a scornful laugh. 'Why? For LifeCorp to take it over, and make a fortune into the bargain?'

'Doesn't it belong to you now?' said Eager.

'Since when did a robot own anything?' asked Cedric.

Eager said nothing. Cedric sounded angry and frustrated, just like the BDC4s he had met before. Eager knew that it was because they were troubled by their human memories. Some had destroyed themselves. The rest were reprogrammed. Most of them went to work in private homes, as Cedric had.

After a while, Cedric said, 'You're an unusual robot.'

'Am I?' said Eager. He was tempted to tell Cedric all about himself – how he had started life in a small room at the top of Professor Ogden's house, and then had joined the Bell family to learn about the world. But he said nothing, remembering the professor's advice to be cautious.

An hour later they reached the outskirts of the city. Eager recognized the landmarks of the old professional quarter.

'Thank you very much,' he said, as Orville glided down to the pavement. 'Are you going to the city now?'

'I shall go home,' said Cedric.

'You came all the way here for me?' exclaimed Eager.

'No matter. I was out for a ride and you gave me a direction,' said Cedric.

Eager was sorry to see him go. 'Perhaps we could meet again? I shall be here for a while.'

The BDC4 nodded. 'I should like that. What about in a week? Same place, same time?'

Eager looked around to be sure of the spot. 'I shall see you then,' he said.

As Orville became a speck in the sky, Eager thought how wonderful life was. He had only been out in the world for a day and already he had made a friend.

thirteen

Eager set off down Wynston Avenue. The street looked both familiar and strange. Red berries gleamed against the snow-covered trees, and bright flowers studded the white bushes, reminding Eager of the Bell children's birthday cakes.

A cat, stepping on to a lawn to bask in the sun, leapt back from the cold snow.

Many times Eager had made this journey, but always late at night so he wouldn't be spotted. Mr and Mrs Bell always had to wait up for him. He was excited at the prospect of surprising them before dark.

The Ban is over. It doesn't matter who sees me now, he thought.

He came to the bend in the road and there was the Bells' house. The blinds were down, which was strange, as the house would normally lower them at dusk. Eager walked up the path and waited for the house's sensor to recognize him. The front door remained closed.

'House!' he called. 'It's me, Eager. I've come to visit Mr and Mrs Bell.'

Still the door did not open. Eager went to the side of the house to look into the kitchen. The blinds were shut. Eager stepped back from the window, his system in turmoil. Even if the Bells were away, the house would surely let him in!

Eager knew what sorrow was. He had felt it when the Bells' robot, Grumps, was destroyed, and when Professor Ogden once disappeared. Over the years he shared the disappointments and losses of the Bells and their children. But nothing could compare to the feeling he had now. To lose Mr and Mrs Bell without saying goodbye, without thanking them for being his family! Never again to hear Mrs Bell's soft voice, or Mr Bell's little jokes . . .

He ran back to the front door. Someone was coming towards him – Mrs Bell!

'Eager!' she cried. 'We didn't expect you so soon.' She leant forward to kiss him. He felt an intense happiness. This was home. The front door opened and he followed her indoors.

'Hello,' said a honeyed voice.

'Hello, house,' said Eager. 'I thought you would let me in.'

The house said, 'I was somewhat distracted.'

'We were conducting an experiment,' said Mrs Bell. 'Ju saw something strange in the garden this morning. It sounded like Sphere, that ball of light Gavin once saw—'

'Sphere!' exclaimed Eager. 'Was Sphere here?'

'That's what we hoped to find out. We made the house dark and were looking out at the garden. But there's been no sign of it.'

'But I saw Sphere —' began Eager.

The next moment, Mr Bell, Finbar and Ju were noisily greeting him. 'Welcome back!'

'We've been expecting you,' said Mr Bell, 'but we weren't sure how you'd get here.'

'I had a lift,' said Eager. He remembered sadly that he had left Allegra's skis in the snowdrift.

Mr Bell looked as if he might ask a question, but Ju burst in, 'Tell us about Sphere. Grandpa says Professor Ogden built it by accident.'

'Yes,' said Eager. 'He was trying to build something else, and he isn't sure what Sphere is. He says it has quantum properties. It appears to me sometimes, usually when I'm unsure what to do. But Sphere can't have been here this morning. It was with me, in the wood.'

'Then what did I see?' asked Ju. She described again the floating ball.

Eager nodded. 'That's Sphere.'

'No doubt it can travel quickly, if it can pass through matter,' said Mr Bell. 'What time did you both see it?'

'Nine o'clock,' said Ju. 'I looked at my jinn.'

Eager nodded. 'It was just after nine when I got home.'

They looked at each other in amazement.

'Are there two Spheres?' asked Mrs Bell.

'I think I would know if there were,' said Eager.

Finbar said tentatively, 'Can the ball appear in two places at once?'

His friends looked at him in silent wonder.

'Now that would be astonishing,' said Mr Bell.

Mrs Bell led the way to the living-room. 'Come and sit down, Eager. Tell us your news.'

'What about ours?' said Ju, throwing herself into a chair. She said in a rush, 'Mum and Dad are away, because Professor Ogden has closed his lab . . .'

Eager nodded.

'. . . and Uncle Gavin and Marcia are getting married!'

The robot took a moment to understand this.

Mrs Bell said, 'I think Eager is as surprised as the rest of us. It's very sudden, isn't it?'

Eager didn't think it was at all sudden. Marcia was Fleur's best friend, and Gavin had known her since they were all children. 'Why didn't they get married before?' he asked.

Mrs Bell smiled. 'I think they began to see each other in a different light.'

A different light? Eager tried to imagine this. He thought of the wood and how the trees changed in the sunlight. But he didn't think that Mrs Bell meant *real* light. And if Marcia and Gavin, somehow, had seen each other differently, what difference did it make? Why did it lead to marriage?

Eager knew about love. Love was surely the feeling he had had outside the house, when he thought he might never see Mr and Mrs Bell again. He loved the Bell family, and Professor Ogden, and Marcia, and Finbar. He loved his robot family – Allegra and Jonquil. Love was a deep, strong, quiet feeling. But there was a kind of love he would never understand.

He remembered when Fleur met Sam. She grew dreamier than ever, and more stormy. She talked about him all the time, even when he had only just left the room. Like much of human behaviour, this sort of feeling would always confuse him . . .

'Eager, you look so puzzled!' said Ju.

He saw that she was grinning at him.

'I think I need to rest,' he said. 'It's been a busy day.'

Mrs Bell led him upstairs to Charlotte's bedroom. It was full of her possessions, as Charlotte didn't have a home of her own. A familiar teddy bear sat on an armchair. Eager paused at the door, waves of memory coming over him. He had looked after Charlotte for most of her childhood.

'I do miss her,' said Mrs Bell. 'But we'll see her at the wedding. Move her things around if you need to. I'll leave you to rest. You're looking overwhelmed.'

'I am,' said Eager. He sat on the floor, turned down his power, and began to process his thoughts.

fourteen

Eager was surprised how quickly he fell into the rhythm of the Bell family. Under the Ban, he had felt the need to be careful about what he did and where he went.

Now everyone could relax. Mrs Bell was busy with what she mysteriously called 'wedding preparations', but she and Mr Bell took time to chat with Eager. Ju and Finbar invited him for walks, and to visit a museum or gobeyhall. At home he cooked, swept snow aside in the garden, and came and went as he pleased.

It was as if the years had rolled back. Ju looked so much like her mother that at times Eager believed she was the young Fleur, and he had just come to live with them again. But one look at Finbar, who wasn't a bit like Gavin, brought him back to the present.

One evening he returned home and went upstairs to Charlotte's room. Halfway up was a mezzanine, with areas for study and exercise. He heard the voices of Mr and Mrs Bell and the whirr of the running machine.

'We must think of something for him to do,' said Mrs Bell, sounding a bit breathless. 'It's cruel otherwise.'

Eager was about to walk on, when he heard his name.

'Poor Eager,' said Mr Bell. 'When he last lived here, the children were growing up. It was a busy household, with lots for him to do. The children were company for him and he learnt alongside them. But he'll soon get bored with only you and me here.'

As Eager wondered whether to go out of earshot, Mrs Bell replied, 'You're right. He hasn't noticed yet because Ju and Finbar are staying. But the moment they leave . . . He likes architecture. Could he do some work for you?'

'I've been wondering about that,' said her husband. 'But he hasn't the sort of brainpower I need. Now Jonquil – he's a different matter.'

Eager had just decided to make his presence known, when Mrs Bell exclaimed, 'What about philosophy? He's very interested in it. He could go on a course.'

'That would raise a few eyebrows,' said Mr Bell.

Mrs Bell sighed. 'He needs friends. But where is he going to meet robots like him?'

Eager lost his resolve to speak. He turned round and went downstairs. The Bells were right. Life would be lonely and quiet once Ju and Finbar left. Already there was little for him to do in the house. There were lots of jobs in the world, but who would employ an odd-looking robot like him when they had an animat? He remembered Fleur and Gavin choosing their careers. They both enjoyed science, but they weren't sure what to study. They said they wanted to do something worthwhile. Eager wanted to do something useful too. He needed – what was the word? – a *purpose* in life.

How did a robot discover that? Could he go to the learning centre, as the Bell children had done, and do tests to find out? He decided to ask Ju and Finbar. After all, the learning centres were open to everyone, whatever their age and wherever they came from. Perhaps that included robots now, too.

fifteen

The next day was the last of the holiday. Ju and Finbar went upstairs to finish their study plans for the new term. Once Mr and Mrs Bell had left for work, Eager climbed to the mezzanine.

'We were just going to call you,' said Ju, spotting him on the stairs. 'Come and look at this.'

Eager peered over her shoulder at the gobetween screen. A dark-haired man was talking. Behind him stood a variety of robots. It was a long time since Eager had seen robots like himself – ones that didn't look like humans. He stared at them with interest.

'It's a show called *Robot Einstein*,' Ju was saying. 'That's Rick Rhodes. He's looking for the cleverest robot in the country.'

'You'd win hands down, Eager,' said Finbar. 'Wait till you see the contestants . . .'

An unseen audience applauded, and Rick Rhodes held out his hands to silence them. 'Our next contender is Eddie,' he said. 'Eddie is a chess-player. "What's so great about that?" you ask. We all know it doesn't take a genius-robot to play chess. You just need enough computing power. Even a cleaner-clone can play chess . . .'

Finbar made a scoffing noise. 'Cleaner-clones aren't stupid. It takes a lot of intelligence to clean a house properly.'

The presenter continued, 'What makes Eddie different is, he doesn't just *play* chess – he *cheats* at chess!'

There was another round of applause.

Rick Rhodes turned to the nervous-looking woman beside him. 'Your father built Eddie, didn't he? Tell us how Eddie cheats at chess.'

The woman cast her eyes heavenward. 'Oh, he swaps pieces around when you aren't looking. And when you're about to make an important move, he distracts you – hides under the table or makes a funny noise – so you forget what you were going to do.'

Laughter rose from the audience.

'Did your father program Eddie to do this?' asked Rick Rhodes.

'Certainly not,' said the woman. 'He can't have learnt it from us either. None of our family cheated at chess. The ability to cheat just evolved.'

'It just evolved!' exclaimed Rick Rhodes. Unexpectedly, he adopted a serious air. 'That's quite a thought. *True* intelligence can't be taught, it can't be programmed – it evolves.' He swung round to the other robots. 'We'll be watching Eddie play chess later. Now let's meet Wilf – the International Weather Forecaster.'

A round head on a squat body trundled forward.

'According to the technocrats who built him, an ability to predict the weather shows the highest intelligence,' said the presenter. 'Wilf, why is that?'

The robot said, 'Predicting the weather requires formidable computational power. Weather is the prime example of a chaotic system, which is not to say it does not have order, but even the smallest variation in the weather produces significant changes that must all be monitored and taken into account. It requires parallel processing of the highest level—'

'Let me interrupt you,' said Rick Rhodes. 'I understand you're saying that weather is incredibly complex, but there are underlying patterns, if only we have the brainpower to see them. Surely you quantum computers have it taped?'

'Have what taped?' asked Wilf.

'You can take into account all the fluctuations of the weather,' said Rick Rhodes.

'Yes,' said Wilf.

'So, tell us what's wrong with the rainfall,' said the presenter.

A silence fell over the studio.

Wilf was about to speak. Rick Rhodes frowned in concentration. He must have received a remote instruction, for he said quickly, 'Sorry, we have to move on. Show us your satellite receptor device . . .'

There were stirrings from the audience but Wilf had obediently turned his head into a screen on which images of Earth from space were appearing.

Finbar sat back in disgust. 'I suppose the producers shut Wilf up in case he was too complicated for the audience.'

'They should let the audience decide,' said Ju. 'I'm always asking Mum and Dad to explain things. I don't understand everything, but I get the general idea.'

'Same here,' said Finbar. 'Not that anyone can explain how you work, Eager.'

Eager said, 'Do you want me to go on the show?'

He looked so horrified that Ju bit her lip to stop herself laughing. 'Of course not,' she managed to say. 'You may be out of hiding, but Professor Ogden must still want you to lie low. He wouldn't have gone away and closed his lab otherwise. You can't appear on a game show.'

The robot looked relieved.

'I wonder what the prize is, though,' said Finbar.

'What is it for?' asked Eager.

'What is what for?' said Finbar.

'The show.'

Ju frowned. 'I don't think it's for anything. It's just entertainment.'

'Oh,' said Eager. Then he remembered his mission. 'I wanted to ask for your help.'

'Switch off gobey,' said Ju. 'Sit down, Eager, and tell us.'

Eager perched awkwardly on the edge of the desk. He was not sure how to begin. 'I can't go on being a visitor here any longer,' he said. 'I want to discover what to do in life.'

Ju and Finbar exchanged a quick glance. Neither of them was experienced in advising robots.

Finbar said thoughtfully, 'I think I know how you feel. We have to make decisions like that as we grow up. It's all very well being free to do what you want, but it's hard to know, isn't it?'

'Especially if you're a robot,' said Eager, sadly.

Ju chewed her lip. 'My dad says the most important thing in life is to keep moving.'

'That's the sort of thing my dad would say,' said Finbar.

Eager looked even sadder. 'Move where?'

'It means don't get stuck,' said Ju. 'Even if you don't know what to do, do something! Anything!'

Eager stared at her.

Finbar said, 'You don't know what you want to do with your life, Eager. So just start with now. What do you want to do today, or tomorrow, or next week?'

'I don't always know what I want to do tomorrow,' said the

robot. 'I like to follow whatever is happening.'

'There must be something in your mind,' said Finbar. 'A place you want to visit, a subject you want to learn, even a question . . .'

'I have a question! I want to know what happened to the stream.' He told them about the wood and the dried-up water.

Ju murmured, 'Like the rivers and lakes around the world. They're drying up and nobody knows why.'

Finbar rocked back on his chair, laughing. 'Well done, Eager! Of all the questions, in all the world, you pick the one no one can answer.'

Ju glared at him. This was no time for teasing. 'If you come to the learning centre, Eager, you can talk about the water problem with real experts on the gobey . . .'

She broke off, imagining herself surrounded by curious students, jostling to get close to Eager, and wondered how she would explain about him to her friends.

Finbar must have read her face. 'Why don't I say that Eager is my robot? People are going to be curious about me, anyway. I'm used to being the new boy and having people stare.' This wasn't strictly true, as Finbar hated being the centre of attention. But he was keen to help Eager. 'What do you think?' he asked the robot.

Eager nodded. 'I think it's a good idea.'

'Come with us tomorrow, then,' said Ju.

sixteen

When she lived at home in the city, Ju was able to walk to the learning centre. But from her grandparents' house in the suburbs, it was a long hoverbus ride. On the way, Ju and Finbar compared their study plans, and Eager thought of questions about the stream.

The hoverbus dropped them a few streets away. As they joined the flow of people from other directions, Ju exclaimed, 'What's going on?'

For Eager wasn't the only robot. Short, bulky, lumbering, wiry – all kinds of robots were striding along beside the students. There were a few animats too.

'No one told me robots were the latest accessory,' said Ju.

'You mean, I'm fashionable?' said Finbar, who had no interest in clothes or trends. 'To think we were worried you'd stand out in a crowd, Eager!'

The robot said nothing. He was busy eyeing the other robots, wondering whether he might make a friend.

Ju whispered incredulously, 'Have all these robots been in hiding too?'

An older boy glanced at Ju as he passed. 'Nice robot!' he called. She felt her cheeks burn and was furious with herself. What would she have done if he'd paid her a personal compliment – fainted?

'You're certainly the most interesting robot here,' Finbar told Eager.

A friend of Ju caught up with them. She was walking with an animat, an early model that looked like an antique doll. 'Isn't this wonderful? Daisy is carrying my bags, and then I'm sending her shopping. She can show me pictures on my jinn and I'll tell her what to buy – that should liven up History!'

'She's never come here before,' said Ju.

'Of course not,' said the girl. 'Mum and Dad wouldn't let her out of the house in case she was arrested for being self-aware. What a joke – my goldfish is more conscious than Daisy!'

Ju laughed too, relieved to have an explanation for the sudden appearance of so many robots.

They crossed the forecourt to the learning centre. It was several storeys high, with semi-translucent walls. Shadowy figures could be seen moving up and down, like ants in a colony. Finbar wondered who would design such a thing, and was glad it had not been Mr Bell. They entered under a large sign: *Centre for Lifelong Learning and Achievement*.

The students formed a queue in reception to register. When they reached the desk, a large eye bent towards them: 'Retinogram, please,' it said, looking into their eyes. Then, 'Identity confirmed.'

'Study plans, please,' said the animats behind the desk.

Finbar followed Ju's example, and held out his arm. The receptionist scanned his jinn with her hand.

'You're a new student,' she said. 'You must talk to the Head of Studies first. Her office is down there.' The animat pointed to a bright blue corridor.

As the students filed out, a girl broke away from her companions and caught Ju's arm: 'There you are! It's *so* good to see you again!' although they had spoken on their jinns only the previous night.

'Hi, Luisa,' said Ju. She noticed that the other girls were gawping at Finbar.

'Who's your friend?' whispered Luisa.

'My cousin,' Ju said loudly, for the benefit of the girls. She would explain to Luisa later.

'I've registered you for this great class,' said Luisa. 'Come on, you'll enjoy it.'

Luisa was always introducing Ju to a traditional craft of some kind or other. Ju gave Finbar and Eager a rueful look as she was led away.

'We'll meet back here,' called Finbar. He set off down the corridor, followed by Eager.

'I'll explain that you're my personal robot and ask if you can stay with me all day,' said Finbar. A door opened at his approach.

'I'll wait outside,' said Eager.

He sat down on a bench. There was a gobetween screen on the opposite wall but he didn't activate it. He preferred to look around. But the corridor was very quiet.

Then a burly animat strode by. He was dressed curiously in what looked like a skirt. The thick patterned fabric hung to his knees. His white shirt had a ruffled front.

'Good morning,' said Eager.

'Morning,' said the animat, walking on.

Five minutes later, a woman bustled towards Eager. 'Thank goodness you're here,' she panted. 'Though I expected an animat. You're not exactly dressed for the part. Now follow me.' She turned on her heels.

Eager hurried after her. 'There's been some mistake. I'm waiting for a student.'

'No!' the woman called, over her shoulder. 'The student is waiting for *you*.'

Eager was unsure whether to protest again. Perhaps Finbar had left by another door and she was taking Eager to him. He followed her past the reception desk and through a wide entrance.

'Here's the extra man,' announced the woman. 'Though I was hoping for an animat.'

Eager stared in astonishment. He was in a gobeyhall. Dozens of students, of all ages, were gazing back at him. He scanned their faces, looking for Finbar.

The woman clapped her hands. 'Now find your partners, everyone. Who volunteers to go with . . . What's your name, robot?'

Before Eager could reply, a girl's voice called, 'I do!'

It was Ju. Grabbing Eager by the arm, she hissed, 'Just follow me.'

The woman stepped on to a podium at the end of the hall. On the gobetween screen behind her, a small band of musicians was assembling. She began, 'Today's dance is the most famous of Scottish dances . . .' Eager did not attend to the rest. He was too busy trying to line up with Ju behind the other couples.

'Wrong side,' said Ju, swapping places with him. 'You're the man. It's easier. I have to move on, but you don't.'

Eager had no idea what she meant. To confuse matters further, more people appeared on the gobetween screens on the walls. The women wore long dresses, with a strip of checked fabric over one shoulder. The men had skirts in the same material – just like the animat that Eager had met in the corridor.

'Ju, there's been a mistake,' he said quietly.

'Of course there has,' whispered Ju. 'But let's not draw attention to ourselves now.'

'The dancers on the gobey screens will demonstrate the steps,' called the woman from the podium. 'If you get lost, just look to the side and copy them.'

The skirted men and women paired up. They crossed arms and held hands. Eager and Ju copied them. The violins struck up. The dancers stepped forwards, turned, and walked backwards.

Eager said with relief, 'This is easy.'

'It gets faster,' said Ju.

They repeated the steps. All of a sudden, Ju was holding Eager by the shoulder and hand, and quickly spinning him round. 'Next time, you lead,' she breathed.

'Lead what?' asked Eager.

'You hold *my* hand and guide us,' said Ju.

But when Eager took her hand, Ju pulled away. He stretched the rubber rings of his arms to hold on to her. A woman skipped into his stretched arm, bounced off, and fell to the floor. The girl behind tripped over her.

'STOP!' cried the woman. The dancers and musicians on the gobetween stopped. 'What is that robot doing?'

'Sorry, it was my fault,' called Ju.

'Go back to your first partner, everyone, and start again,' said the woman.

The musicians struck up once more. Eager clasped Ju's hand as they spun round. 'Now let go,' said Ju. 'I'm supposed to move on!'

Eager stood there, bewildered, until another girl took Ju's place. 'Get moving,' she said. They paced forwards and backwards and it was time to twirl around. Eager remembered to let go of his partner. A thin woman took her place. 'Not too fast,' she said. 'I haven't danced in ages.'

But it was hard not to dance fast. The music seemed to be getting quicker. The boy and girl in front of them stumbled. A new partner came to Eager. It was Ju's friend, Luisa. Instead of striding, they had to take mincing steps to fit in all the moves.

His next partner was red in the face and breathless. The music was faster than ever and Eager was running, where before he had walked. He just managed to keep his footing during the spin.

On the screen, a bearded man was dancing so quickly that his legs became a blur. He barged into the man in front, knocking him over. That man collapsed on to the next, and like a line of dominoes every man fell flat on his face. The women carried on dancing, twirling around with empty arms.

Another couple careered into Eager and his partner. Unlike the dancers on the screen, they were fast-moving muscle and bone.

'Ouch!' cried the red-faced girl, as she and Eager toppled

over. The couple behind would have squashed them, but Eager rolled away, pulling the girl with him. Extending his arms, he swung her, screaming, into the air and landed her safely by the door.

The woman on the podium shouted at the gobetween to stop, but the violins played on, ever faster, as all the dancers fell into a heap. Eager worked quickly to untangle flailing limbs and pull people to their feet. The violins gave a final shriek. Eager looked around at the stunned dancers, and noticed the woman carving her way towards him. Several voices cried pleadingly, 'It wasn't the robot's fault!'

The wide doors opened and a well-dressed man entered. Ju made her way to Eager. 'That's the Principal,' she whispered. 'Leave any talking to me.'

seventeen

Finbar was waiting in the reception area, wondering where Eager had gone. Several students went by, limping or nursing bruises. He watched in bemusement as they followed a sign marked *First Aid*.

Ju and the robot appeared soon afterwards. 'There you are!' he said. 'The good news is, you can stay with me, Eager. But the other robots can't come into the learning centre – there are too many of them.'

'Why does Eager get special treatment?' asked Ju.

Finbar grinned. 'The Head of Studies is a fan of Mum's paintings. She assumed Mum must be very rich and that Eager is my bodyguard.'

'Oh,' said Ju. 'Well, we may all be sent home anyway. The simulation generator keeps breaking down. The Principal said they tried to fix it over the holidays, but it still isn't right. Our dance lesson just ended in chaos. Twenty Scottish dancers in full tartan were too much for it.'

It's a shame if we have to go home,' said Finbar. 'Eager was hoping to ask about the water problem.' He noticed the robot's crestfallen face. 'Why don't we go and find out now, if the simulator is still working? I know where the gobeyrooms are.'

'I'm going to Biomechanics,' said Ju. 'I'll meet you for lunch in the canteen. Top floor.'

Finbar and Eager hurried to the lifts. 'How did you get to be at a dance class?' the boy asked.

Eager had just finished his story by the time they reached the ninth floor. 'Good job you're mainly rubber,' laughed Finbar. 'Anyone falling on you would bounce.'

They came to a row of cubicles and entered the nearest. There was no door. 'It must have an acoustic barrier,' said Finbar. 'I'll just check.' He went outside, leaving Eager behind.

'Did you hear anything?' asked Finbar, poking his head round the cubicle.

'Nothing,' said Eager.

'Good. You won't be overheard. I'll go next door and see what I can find out,' said Finbar.

Eager faced the screen on the far wall. 'I should like to speak to an expert on water,' he said.

'Can you be more precise?' said the gobetween. 'Do you mean an expert on the waterways, the water supply, the water cycle, or the chemical composition of water?'

Eager was thrown by the questions. None of them seemed

to fit his problem. 'I should like to find out where the stream in the wood has gone,' he said.

'I recommend a dowser,' said the gobetween. 'One moment.'

A sad-faced man appeared. Dressed for wet weather, he was sitting on a garden terrace. Eager switched himself to simulation mode and joined him.

'How can I help?' asked the man.

Eager explained about the stream. 'The snow had begun to melt, so I expected some water to flow,' he said. 'But the stream-bed remained dry.'

The man nodded. 'I expect it became blocked somehow. Many things can cause a blockage. Fallen stones, a block of ice that is slow to melt . . .'

Eager looked up at the sky. There were no clouds. He wondered why the man was dressed as he was. 'Is it going to rain?' he asked.

'Yes,' said the man.

'You must be right about the stream,' said Eager. 'Will the blockage move?'

'In time,' said the dowser, 'depending on the cause.' He added, 'There is another possibility.'

Eager waited to hear more, but the man just looked gloomily at him. 'Please tell me,' said the robot.

'It may have died,' said the man.

Died? Eager knew that water could disappear by evaporating. And it could freeze or become steam. But he had never heard of water dying.

'Rivers die,' said the man. 'Pollution removes the oxygen and they can no longer sustain life. Plants and fish are no more. But recently I've been finding that water can vanish for no apparent reason. I believe it loses the will to live.'

Eager was astonished. The dowser was talking as if water was a person! He tried to recall any signs that the stream had been unhappy. All he could remember was the way it bubbled into the open and the gurgling sounds it made.

'I think the stream was joyful,' he said.

'That's just it,' said the man. For a moment there was a glimmer of passion in his eyes. 'There's no reason for all this water vanishing. I'm being asked more and more to find lost sources of water. That's why I have to believe it's going to rain. Although, in my heart, I don't think rain is the answer.'

Eager was beginning to wonder about the question, let alone the answer. 'Thank you for your help,' he said hastily. 'Perhaps we could talk again one day.'

The sorrowful man and the terrace disappeared. Eager went into the corridor where Finbar joined him.

'Any luck?' asked the boy.

'I learnt some things,' said Eager, 'but I'm not sure they were the answer to my question.'

'Same here,' said Finbar. 'I was just told loads of facts and figures. Let's go and meet Ju.'

eighteen

The canteen was on the rooftop. All the surfaces were titanium, and for a moment Finbar felt like a carrot in a saucepan. Fake trees brushed against the silver walls. He looked out of the window on to frost-covered playing fields.

Ju had kept a table for them. 'Did you enjoy your morning, Eager?' she asked. 'Apart from the dance fiasco.'

Eager was aghast. Had he only been at the learning centre for a morning? It felt like a whole day – a very long day. 'I've had an interesting time,' he said politely. 'I met a friendly man on the gobetween. He thinks that water has lost the will to live.'

Ju and Finbar exchanged baffled glances.

A voice said, 'Hello, may I have a word?'

Ju swung round. 'Mrs Newton!'

It was the teacher from the dancing class. Ju smiled brightly, wondering whether she was in trouble after all.

'It's about your robot,' said Mrs Newton.

Eager recalled the way she had marched towards him, and sank deeper into his seat.

'He's with me, actually,' said Finbar. 'He's my bodyguard.'

'Well, at least he's stronger than he looks,' said Mrs Newton. 'But it's his brain I'm interested in. Perhaps I was a little hasty in my judgement. The other students have been telling me how quick he was to help them, and how carefully he behaved. May I sit down?' She took the seat next to Ju, facing Eager and Finbar. 'We're very grateful to him. People could have been seriously hurt, but in the end no bones were broken.'

'Don't you want to thank Eager?' said Ju. 'He understands, just like us.'

'Why, naturally!' said the woman, although she didn't sound natural as she said, 'Thank you, Eager.'

'Not at all, Mrs Newton,' said the robot.

She turned to Finbar. 'He seems very bright and good at taking the initiative. Have you thought of entering him . . .' Something in Finbar's eye stopped her. She switched her gaze to Eager. 'Have you thought of entering the *Robot Einstein* competition?'

'No,' said Eager.

Mrs Newton said coaxingly, 'You came to the rescue this morning. Wouldn't you like to help save the world?'

'Save the world?' echoed Eager, his suspicions raised. He had met people before who believed the world needed saving. Their plans usually involved him doing something he didn't want to do.

'Perhaps that's exaggerating,' said Mrs Newton hastily. 'But there's no doubt that the rainfall problem is serious. Very serious indeed.'

'Excuse me, Mrs Newton,' said Finbar. 'What has the weather got to do with *Robot Einstein*?'

'Don't you know?' she asked. 'Lifecorp is sponsoring the show. The winners will form a think-tank, to come up with answers to the problem.'

Ju said, 'Isn't the show just for fun?'

'Oh no, not this time,' said the teacher. She settled herself into her seat. 'You know about the Ban, do you?'

Ju frowned as if thinking hard, and noticed that Finbar was doing the same. She suppressed a smile. 'Um, yes, my dad explained it to me,' she said.

'It's had a terrible affect on science. Stifled research and put people off becoming technocrats. There is a shortage of scientists, and the most talented people have turned to other things. So who is going to solve the weather problem?'

Mrs Newton paused for breath. 'Weather is notoriously hard to understand, in any case. We might model it on our computers, but how do we interpret the data? There's the rub. And then what do we do to solve things?'

Finbar said, 'You were talking about the Ban.'

She lowered her voice. 'During the Ban, a lot of intelligent robots were kept out of sight, in case they were accused of being self-aware. Now it's safe for them again. Of course, no one believes they can be conscious, but they just might be clever enough to solve our problems, especially if they have an understanding of human needs – like our friend here.' She beamed at Eager.

'Now Eager, were you to enter and win, you would join the robot think-tank. The head of robotics at LifeCorp is going to train you to work together . . .'

She was talking as if Eager had already entered and won. The robot said, 'I shall have to think about it.'

Mrs Newton stood up to leave. 'Let me know, won't you, Eager?'

'But why have a competition?' asked Ju. 'LifeCorp could just ask on the gobetween if anyone has an intelligent robot.'

Mrs Newton burst out laughing. 'I believe they did mention it – and the public was only too glad to help. LifeCorp was flooded with details of robots that impersonated the family pet, played the drums or made excellent apple pie . . .'

Eager remembered that he made good pancakes. The Bells seemed to think it was a valuable skill. Mrs Newton was still talking: 'Imagine sifting through that lot! So LifeCorp had the idea of using the game show, and having expert judges decide whether the robots really are exceptionally intelligent or not.'

'You seem to know a lot about the competition,' said Finbar.

Unexpectedly, the teacher looked coy. 'As a matter of fact, I'm on the panel of judges. When I'm not teaching traditional dance – which is a passion of mine – I teach psychology. Well, goodbye Eager. Perhaps I'll see you on the show.'

After she had left, Ju and Finbar became aware of the buzz of conversation around them. 'I think they're talking about us,' whispered Ju.

Eager saw several pairs of eyes upon him. He was used to being an object of curiosity, but what would it be like to appear on the gobetween before millions?

'What do you want to do this afternoon, Eager?' asked Finbar.

The robot gathered his thoughts. 'I'd like a quiet time. I think I'll listen to a story.'

nineteen

Eager returned to the ninth floor. The students he passed were busy chatting and hardly noticed him. Entering the cubicle he had used that morning, he switched himself to simulation mode. He was keen to hear the myth that Professor Ogden had mentioned. 'Gobetween, I would like to know the story of Prometheus,' he said.

The temperature in the cubicle dropped. Judging from the light, it was late afternoon. Eager was surrounded by sky, until he looked down and saw rows of miniature trees, swaying in the wind. Ahead of him, tiny people squatted on the ground. They were huddled together; he guessed for warmth and shelter from the wind.

He looked around, and finding no one else to talk to, bent down to the people. As his shadow loomed above them, they screamed and cowered against the ground. Some held out their arms beseechingly. He heard a cry: 'Oh, Lord Prometheus. Help us!'

Eager addressed the young girl who had called out. 'I'm not Prometheus,' he said crossly. He had had enough of mistaken identity for one day.

'Lord Prometheus, do not jest with us!' cried the girl. 'You fashioned us out of clay and breathed air into us to give us life. We are grateful to you. But see how we suffer! We have nothing to warm us in the cold night air; we have no protection from the wild animals and we eat our meat raw, as they do.'

Eager noticed how cold and wretched she and her companions looked, and felt pity for them. 'I'm sorry to hear that,' he said.

'Don't be sorry,' said the girl. 'You can help us. Bring us fire from the gods.'

Eager tilted his head, wondering how he might do that. There were screams again as people flattened themselves to the ground in terror.

'Don't worry – I'm only thinking,' said Eager. 'I can't eat you, even if I wanted to. How do I bring you fire?'

The girl leapt to her feet and pointed behind her. 'You go to the top of Mount Olympus, where the gods reside, and bring it back.'

The mountain was high, but Eager saw no reason why he shouldn't climb it. 'Is that all?' he asked.

The girl nodded. She seemed not to breathe as she waited for his response.

'Very well,' said Eager. 'I shall bring you fire.'

So as not to scare them again, he was careful to step around the people and not over them. When he looked back they had risen to their feet. Some gave him a melancholy wave.

Eager began to feel apprehensive. The mountain, which he reached in a few strides, had an unwelcoming air. He started to climb. The grassy lower slopes gave way to rocks and craggy overhangs. He slithered and slipped until he thought of extending his rubber limbs. Once he became even more of a giant, it took a matter of minutes to reach the summit.

The air was warm and still. Golden pillars, encircled with vines, rose up ahead of him. Even more golden was a chariot that reminded him of Cedric's flying machine. Four magnificent horses were tethered nearby. As he approached, Eager saw that the chariot's golden glow was a fire that never consumed it. He couldn't take a chariot down the mountain – it was far too big and would burn him terribly. How could he transport its fire?

A boy in a short white tunic passed. He was carrying a large silver jug, studded with jewels, on a silver tray. His lips were pursed as he concentrated on keeping his balance.

'Excuse me,' said Eager.

The boy gave a start, and the silver jug wobbled.

'Zeus will punish me if I spill his wine!' said the boy.

Eager recognized the name from other myths he had heard. 'Isn't Zeus the chief god?' he asked.

The boy nodded. 'And you're Prometheus, who made the race of mortals,' he said.

Eager gave up arguing about his identity. 'I'd like to take a bit of fire down to them,' he said.

The boy shrank back against a pillar. 'The wrath of Zeus . . .' he began, his eyes round with terror. 'He's forbidden you to do that.'

'Has he?' said Eager. 'That seems unfair. It's very cold down there at night.'

'If mortals have fire, they will challenge the gods,' said the boy. 'They will want all this . . .' Eager followed his gaze beyond the pillars and saw an enormous golden palace.

'Humans like their comforts,' Eager agreed. 'At the moment they eat their food raw, which is boring. Fire will give them variety.' He imagined helping Mrs Bell in the kitchen. 'They will be able to grill, bake, steam, roast, boil . . .'

'That's enough cookery,' said the boy, putting down the tray. 'If you must take fire, here's a fennel-stalk to carry it in.'

He handed Eager a large stem that was hollow inside. Eager found a fallen branch and thrust it at the fiery chariot. Now he had a burning torch. He smothered it on the ground with a handful of damp moss to put out the flame and broke off an ember, which he dropped into the hollow stalk.

Eager turned to thank the boy; but he had gone, taking his tray.

The robot scrambled down the mountain, holding his precious cargo. As he lowered the fennel-stalk to the ground, ten tiny people rushed forward and took it from him.

'Inside is a burning ember for you to light a fire,' he said.

Sounds of an explosion filled the air. The little people crouched behind the stalk. Eager ducked too but there was nowhere for a giant to hide.

'Zeus's thunderbolt!' cried the young girl, as a second blast rent the air.

'Prometheus!' roared a voice. 'You have given fire to the mortals, and you will be punished!'

'What happens now?' asked Eager.

The girl said, 'You're chained to a mountain in the cold and frost, and every night a vulture plucks out your liver. By day it grows back again.'

It was small comfort to Eager that he didn't have a liver. He decided it was time to go, and quickly switched out of simulation mode.

twenty

Mr and Mrs Bell were watching the gobetween screen that had recently been installed in the living-room. They looked round as Eager and the children filed into the room.

'Excuse us for a moment,' said Mrs Bell, her attention still on the screen. It showed a view of Earth from space.

A voice was saying, 'Our planet is blue, but for how much longer? Governments suffered a setback today in their plans to lower the Earth's temperature. Speaking at a conference in Mexico City, scientists said there has been no temperature increase to account for the droughts across the world. Governments had planned to open the giant sunshades that earlier scientists placed above the Earth to cool the planet. These umbrellas saved us in the past from the global warming that threatened our survival. But scientists today said that opening the shades again risked cooling the planet unnecessarily . . .'

The picture changed and Mr Bell said, 'Gobey, switch off. Well, that wasn't very helpful. How was your day?'

'OK, thanks,' said Ju. 'But what exactly do these sunshades do? They don't block the sun completely, do they?'

'That would be fatal,' said Mr Bell. 'No, they're giant filters that reduce the amount of sunlight reaching the earth. It's a risky business because we never know the knock-on consequences.'

'There's more to these droughts than meets the eye,' said Mrs Bell.

'The problem is, it isn't raining,' said Finbar. 'Isn't that right?'

'That's true, but I think some governments are making matters worse,' said Mrs Bell. 'They must be diverting rivers or secretly drawing water from lakes.' She sighed. 'We had these problems years ago. We thought the technocrats had solved them.'

Ju gave Eager an encouraging glance. The robot said, 'I'd like to ask you something. Mrs Newton wants me to enter the *Robot Einstein* competition . . .'

'Mrs Newton?' queried Mrs Bell.

'A teacher at the learning centre. She's one of the judges,' said Ju. 'Do you know about the show, Gran?'

Mrs Bell worked part-time for LifeCorp, the show's sponsor. 'Oh yes,' she said. 'There's been a big fuss about it at work. There are contests all over the world and the winners are supposed to work together on the weather problem. But I never thought for a moment you might want to go on it, Eager.'

'Mrs Newton thinks I might be able to help,' said the robot.

'Aren't they looking for number wizards?' asked Mr Bell. 'You know, robots that can do huge calculations at the speed of light? More Allegra's line, I should have thought.'

'But she doesn't know anything about the world,' said Eager. 'Mrs Newton says that would be my contribution.'

'And, it would be an opportunity for you to meet other robots,' said Mrs Bell.

Eager nodded. Since seeing the robots at the learning centre that morning, he had been hoping for exactly that.

Ju bit her lip. 'But Professor Ogden has closed his lab and gone away to avoid any publicity. Now you're thinking of appearing in front of millions of people.'

'And of going to LifeCorp,' added Mrs Bell. 'Though anyone who might recognize Eager has left LifeCorp. No one need know that Professor Ogdon built him.'

'But don't you think we should ask the professor first?' persisted Ju.

'He said he can't be contacted,' said Eager, tilting his head. 'Perhaps I shouldn't enter, after all.' Part of him was relieved at the thought, but he still longed to meet other robots and to try to solve the problem of his stream. 'Couldn't I just join the think-tank without going on the show?'

Finbar leant forward. 'Remember what Mrs Newton said? LifeCorp won't take any robot just because it volunteers. Being on the show is part of the selection process.'

Ju frowned. 'Why not just hire the judges to choose the most intelligent robots? Why bother having a competition?'

'But how would you find the robots?' asked Finbar. 'If you made a big appeal on the gobetween people might panic . . .'

Ju cried, 'That's what the International Space Authority said last year about the strange signal that Dad witnessed. "We can't tell the public – they may panic!" But surely people should know the truth?'

'But what *is* the truth?' asked Mrs Bell. 'We heard on the news that scientists can't agree. Years ago things were different. It became clear that we could stop global warming. We used new technology and stopped being so wasteful. This time, no one seems to know what to do.'

Although he was trying to follow the conversation, Eager felt bemused. He liked to ask questions too. But humans often discussed things as if they were unravelling a mystery. It had taken him years to understand that people could mean something different to what they had said.

Mr Bell said, 'I think Finbar's right. LifeCorp doesn't want to admit it can't solve the problems. It hasn't produced any intelligent robots for years, because of the Ban, so it's using *Robot Einstein* as a way of getting the public involved. No one will get too alarmed because it's just a show; on the other hand, it's for a serious purpose, so people will want to help.'

Eager looked gratefully at Mr Bell. If he agreed with Mrs Newton that the show was worthwhile, Eager would be doing the right thing to appear on it. He would meet other robots and, more importantly, find a purpose – he would help solve the problem of the drought. It was just the opportunity he had been looking for!

Professor Ogden could hardly disapprove. Besides, he had said that Eager must make his own choices. 'I shall enter the competition,' the robot said firmly.

The rest of the conversation stopped.

'I'm sure you'll enjoy it,' said Mrs Bell.

'I'll tell Mrs Newton tomorrow,' said Ju.

Later that evening, as Eager helped Mrs Bell cook supper, she remarked, 'Do you know, you've been here a week? Usually this would be your last evening. But now the Ban is lifted, you can stay as long as you like.'

A week! That meant he was due to meet Cedric tomorrow afternoon. The day had been so eventful that Eager had lost track of time. He noticed that Mrs Bell was looking hurt, and realized he had not replied to her. 'Thank you, Mrs Bell. I should like to stay with you for longer.'

'As long as you like. You're part of the family, Eager. Don't forget that, whatever happens.'

'I won't,' said Eager.

twenty-one

The next morning Eager was ready to explain that he couldn't go to the learning centre. But as he laid the toast on the dining-room table, Ju said, 'Bad news, Eager. The simulation generator at the learning centre has finally broken down. We all have to study at home today.'

'Oh,' said Eager. 'I have an engagement this afternoon, in any case.'

Finbar smiled at him. 'That's lucky.'

The family began to discuss arrangements for the day, leaving Eager feeling out of sorts. He realized he was disappointed that no one had asked about his engagement. He would have liked to mention that he was meeting a friend.

Ju looked up from her toast. 'I won't forget to call Mrs Newton. You're still sure you want to enter *Robot Einstein*?'

'Yes,' said Eager, who had spent much of the night thinking about his new mission.

The children went upstairs to study. Eager had offered to

help Mrs Bell with the chores and was keen to get everything done before going to meet Cedric. Unlike the previous day, time seemed to crawl. At last it was the afternoon.

It was a cool, blustery day. Grey patches of snow still hung around the gardens. Eager hurried to the spot where Orville had dropped him the previous week. He could hardly contain his excitement as a golden speck descended from the sky. He remembered the fiery chariot on the mountain and thought of poor Prometheus, chained to his rock. If all gods were as vengeful as Zeus, it was a good thing they no longer existed.

The instant he landed, Cedric climbed out and shook Eager's hand. 'Hop in, then we can talk,' he said.

They flew over the old technocrats' quarter and cut across the motorway that was teeming with hovercars. Soon there was nothing but woods and fields, edged with white snow. Cedric chatted about the flying machine, describing technical details that Eager only half understood.

They swooped down towards a river, meandering through meadows of summer flowers. 'Just like the countryside used to be,' said Cedric. 'They keep it like this for the city-dwellers to visit.'

Orville landed on a flat rock and the robots began to walk beside the river. Eager was delighted to be in the country again. He realized he was missing the wood by his home in the hillside.

'How are you, Eager?' asked Cedric.

Eager told him about his week. Cedric laughed uproariously when he heard about the dancing lesson. 'I should like to dance,' he added, unexpectedly.

'And I may appear on *Robot Einstein*,' said Eager.

'That fool show?' retorted Cedric.

Eager was taken aback. He explained to the BDC4 about the shortage of technocrats, and how LifeCorp was trying to find robots to help solve the weather problem.

Cedric said scornfully, 'Never mind the Ban. We're short of technocrats because LifeCorp hasn't trained any. It's been too busy raking in the money from those empty-headed animats. LifeCorp runs just about everything on this planet. It only cares about profit, never mind our survival.'

This time Eager was speechless. He knew that the Bells did not always approve of LifeCorp, but he had never heard anyone make Cedric's claims.

Of course, it was no surprise that Cedric should dislike LifeCorp. The company had carried out a dangerous experiment in giving him a dead person's memories. And it had not helped the BDC4s when their human minds caused them confusion . . . Eager had a new thought. Surely Cedric had forgotten these things when he was reprogrammed at the factory?

Before he could ask more, Cedric said, 'I think we must beg to differ.'

'Yes,' said Eager.

'I shall watch the show, nonetheless,' continued Cedric. 'To lend my support.'

'Perhaps I could get you a ticket,' said Eager excitedly.

The robot's jaw set firm. 'I don't go out in public,' he said.

They walked on in silence. A kingfisher dived into the river ahead of them. Eager said brightly, 'Do you know the myth of Prometheus?'

'I do,' said Cedric. 'It tells how fire separated us from the rest of nature.'

'Us?' said Eager, confused.

Cedric said hastily, 'I mean humans, of course, but robots too.'

'How?' asked Eager.

Cedric assumed a dramatic tone. 'Once humans had fire, other animals were kept at bay. They sat behind their wall of heat, watching the animals' eyes gleam in the firelight. With fire we learnt to conquer our fellow creatures, and later our fellow humans.'

Eager imagined the tiny people, no longer shivering on the plain, watching the fire and thinking themselves gods.

'Fire gave humans a technological advantage,' Cedric went on. 'Now they could transform the raw materials of nature.'

He scooped mud from the riverbank and held it out to Eager. 'Clay – they heated it to make pots, then bricks to build houses, bridges and roads; earthenware pipes to carry water; jewellery and sculptures to offer to the gods.'

He dropped the mud and picked up a stone, turning it in his hand. 'They melted rocks to extract the ore, and forged the metal into weapons and tools. Using heat, they learnt to make stronger and harder metals. Eventually they pulled it into wires to conduct electricity.'

Eager listened, as rapt as when he visited the theatre. He realized that Cedric was giving him a swift history of the humans' world.

Cedric scrambled down the riverbank, returning with a handful of fine stones. 'Sand!' He let it trickle through his slender fingers. 'Fire turned sand into glass. We made drinking vessels and windows; then telescopes and microscopes – turning the world inside out and showing us the stars! Then optical fibres to run our computers, and finally us.' He looked at Eager. 'It's thanks to fire that we exist. Scarcely a part of us could be made without fire.'

Eager contemplated his body, something he had not done since he was first built. It was true – his metal, his rubber, the circuitry and quantum processors inside him – all depended on great heat.

'Animals certainly couldn't keep up with that,' he said.

Cedric threw back his head and laughed. 'But they did – in a way! Humans, for all their achievements, still went at the pace of the animals. Even when they borrowed speed, it was that of the camel or horse. Once they used fire to produce steam and harnessed its power to move their engines, then they left nature behind!'

Eager began to applaud, forgetting that he wasn't sitting in a theatre. Cedric lowered his arms, which he had been waving around as he spoke.

'When I thought about humans having fire, I thought of cooking!' admitted Eager.

The BDC4 gave him a searching look. 'You may have a point,' he said. 'Could cooking food have given us an advantage? What if it altered the brain in some way, so that we acquired higher intelligence? If we were still eating raw meat, would we have gone on to create cities and fine art, and to think about the meaning of life?'

'You mean, would *humans*?' said Eager gently.

'Yes, yes, of course,' said Cedric. 'It's a thought, isn't it?' He looked up at the sun. 'We'd better get back. We don't want your friends to report you missing.'

twenty-two

As he walked along Wynston Avenue, Eager relived the afternoon with satisfaction. Cedric was a real friend. He had been interested in Eager and his news . . . A thought struck him. He had learnt nothing more about Cedric, not even what he had done that week.

Perhaps Cedric was very shy. The more Eager tried to convince himself of this, the more he felt uneasy. He remembered Professor Ogden's last words: 'Conscious and conscience. It's no coincidence that they sound alike.' Was Eager experiencing what the professor had meant? His consciousness told him that Cedric was friendly. But his conscience told him that something was wrong. What he *knew* and what he *felt* were at odds.

That's why truth was so important! If you knew the truth about something, and you were truthful about your feelings, it was easier to make the right decisions in life. And if you didn't know the truth, it was better to be cautious –

just what Professor Ogden had advised him to be.

Eager had reached the house, and saw Ju waving at him from the window. He raised his arm in reply, but Ju's waving grew more frantic. She disappeared from view as he reached the front door.

'Thank goodness!' she cried, running into the hallway. 'We were worried you wouldn't be back in time. You're on the show tonight. A flying pod is coming any minute to collect us!'

'How can I be on the show tonight?' asked Eager. 'I only decided yesterday.'

Ju hopped impatiently. 'Mrs Newton says new entries come in every minute. Hundreds came yesterday from all the robots at the learning centre. She interviews them on the gobey. Then she talks to the other judges and they decide which ones to have on the show. She bumped off a lexicographer for you.'

Before Eager could ask more, Finbar called from the stairs, 'Hi Eager! Ju, does this look all right?'

It seemed to Eager that the boy was wearing a smarter version of his everyday clothes and looked much the same as usual. But Ju perused him for several seconds before giving her approval. As Finbar disappeared upstairs again, she caught the robot's eye. 'He's nervous about appearing in front of millions of people.'

'Which people?' said Eager.

Ju laughed. 'The audience, of course. Mrs Newton thinks

you're Finbar's robot so he'll be introduced as your owner.' She ran into the kitchen, returning with two glasses of water. Eager stood in the hallway, thinking about the 'millions of people'.

'Are Mr and Mrs Bell still at work?' he asked.

'Yes, but Gran says they'll be home in time to watch the show. Marcia and Uncle Gavin are going to be in the audience with us. Rick Rhodes is a friend of Marcia, and we're going to sit in VIP seats.'

Eager brightened up. He would like to see Gavin and Marcia.

The green light by the front door flickered. 'The flying pod is outside,' said the house. 'You had better hurry.'

'Finbar!' Ju shrieked.

The boy scrambled down the stairs and she handed him a glass of water. He finished it in one gulp. 'Thanks, Ju. Come on Eager, let's show them what you can do.'

The pilot was a young man who didn't look much older than Finbar and Ju. 'IDs, please,' he said, scanning their jinns. 'Just to make sure I've got the right robot.' He winked at them. 'Climb in and strap up. Help yourself to refreshments.'

Ju and Finbar looked at the trays of food and drink beside them. There were bottles of water with names like 'Arctic Ice' and 'Mountain Stream'. Were they genuine, Ju wondered? She imagined a bottle called 'Desalted Atlantic Ocean' and decided it would never sell.

Finbar took a lexiscreen from his pocket and unrolled it.

'Supercool!' cried Ju, admiringly. The lexiscreen was as fine as a sheet of writing paper.

The boy handed the lexiscreen to Eager. 'We had to choose a special subject for you. Gavin suggested philosophy. I hope that's all right. I've made a few notes for you.'

Eager read the list of names. 'Thank you, Finbar. I've met several of these philosophers already – Socrates, Plato, Hobbes, Sartre . . . I shall look forward to talking about their views.'

'Wonderful,' said Finbar, with a sideways glance at Ju.

'I'm glad I'm not Rick Rhodes,' she murmured.

The show took place in a gobeyhall in the centre of the city. The flying pod touched down in the street to let out its passengers, and a young woman hurried to meet them.

'I'm Hester. Welcome to *Robot Einstein*.' She ushered them through double doors. 'You're the last to arrive. The other robots are waiting in the green room. I'll quickly show you the ropes then you can join them before the show begins.'

They passed through a corridor illuminated with holograms of past shows. Eager recognized some of the nursery characters from when Charlotte was small. Ju and Finbar couldn't resist pointing them out to each other.

'Did you used to watch that one?'

'I loved that rabbit!'

Wide doors parted to let them into the studio, a surprisingly small space ringed with tiers of seats. Hester said, pointing around the room, 'The judges sit that side. Those seats opposite are for the owners. The robots can sit with you later. You come on from the back, Eager. Don't worry about facing the audience, everyone can see you full-on from the gobey in front of them. They can zoom in on the judges too. They're always arguing, so that's fun.'

Eager had no idea what Hester meant. *What* was he going to be on, and *full* of what? If he was confused now, how would he cope with people, lights and music?

Humans and animats in dark overalls were going to and fro. It wasn't clear what they were doing, but they appeared busy.

Hester said, 'Finbar, do you want to come on with your robot or not?'

Finbar said in surprise, 'Don't I have to?'

'Some owners do,' said Hester. 'Personally I think it's more fun if the robots are on their own. There's another boy here tonight – Dean. He doesn't want to appear on the show.'

'Actually, I'd rather not – unless you want me to, Eager,' said Finbar.

Eager remembered that he was going to discuss philosophy. He recalled his lively conversations with philosophers on the gobetween. 'I shall be all right,' he said. 'I'm looking forward to the show.'

Finbar gave an exaggerated sigh of relief. Ju grinned.

'Any questions?' said Hester briskly.

'Which philosopher shall I meet?' asked Eager.

Hester frowned. 'Which what?'

'Philosophy is Eager's special subject,' said Ju.

'I see. Well we don't have any experts here tonight. But the judges will have consulted them on the gobetween when setting their questions.' Hester led them across the studio floor. 'Let's go backstage. The green room is behind that door.'

Eager wondered why she was so keen to mention the colour scheme. 'Have you just decorated, Hester?' he asked.

'What?' she said.

Eager was wondering whether she was hard of hearing, when Ju hissed, 'The green room is the actors' waiting-room. It's a tradition.' Aloud she said, 'I'd better go and join my uncle and his fiancée.'

'Is that Marcia Morris' party?' said the young woman. 'I'll take you to them. They're in the VIP guest-room.'

'What colour is that?' asked Eager.

Hester glared at him, and he hurried after Finbar into the green room.

twenty-three

The green room was smaller than Eager had expected. There were no windows and it was dimly lit. It had a few armchairs, a gobetween screen, and holographs on the wall. Two contestants stood at the far end, one slender and silver, not unlike a BDC4; the other huge and box-like.

The silver robot came forward. 'Hello, I'm Olga.' Her voice was husky.

'How do you do, Olga? I'm Eager.'

'Eager for what?' asked Olga.

'My name is Eager,' said Eager.

'Eager is an interesting name,' she drawled. 'Tell me about it.'

Eager was delighted by Olga's attention. She seemed very friendly. He said, 'Gavin chose the name for me. I'm an EGR-type robot, and I am eager by nature so—'

'One can be too eager,' interrupted Olga.

Eager reflected. 'I suppose one can.' He thought he would

try a little joke. 'Although *I* can never be too Eager, can I?'

The huge robot came to stand beside Olga. They looked intently at Eager, as he tried to explain. 'I am Eager, so everything about me is Eager.' The robots continued to stare and Eager began to regret his experiment. He said, 'You can't be *too* Olga, can you, Olga?'

'There is only one of me,' said Olga.

'That's true,' said Eager. 'But I didn't mean that kind of two.'

Olga said, 'Didn't you mean "too" too?'

The huge robot pointed his toes and began to sing in a deep voice:

'I've got a tutu, have you got a tutu?
If you've got a tutu too,
Between we two, we've got two tutus.
Two tutus make two.'

He seized Eager by the hands and spun him round. For his bulk, he was surprisingly agile. At last he stopped and said, 'Knock knock.'

It took Eager a moment to get his bearings.

'Knock knock,' repeated the robot.

Eager had played the game many times with Charlotte when she was little. 'Who's there?' he said.

'Wooden shoe.'

Eager looked at the robot's feet. They were clumpy and metal.

'Wooden shoe who?' he said.

'Wooden shoe like to know?' said the robot.

Finbar had backed against the wall during the dance. Now he stepped forward. 'As a matter of fact, I would like to know. Who are you?'

'Wag,' said the robot.

'Wag?' echoed Finbar.

'World Am—'

The robot's reply was drowned out by a booming voice: 'Five minutes.'

Finbar said, 'That means five minutes until the show begins. I'd better go. Relax, Eager.' He winked at him. 'I think you're in with a good chance.'

The door had barely closed on Finbar when it reopened. An animat with red hair came in. 'Olga, you're on,' he said. The silver robot followed him from the room.

'Good luck,' said Eager.

twenty-four

Finbar went along the corridor until he found a door marked *Men*. On his way in, he bumped into a boy coming out. He recoiled and gasped. It was almost like coming face to face with a clone of himself. In a way, he *was* seeing his double. The boy before him was tall and pale-faced, not a bit like Finbar – but the previous summer he had stolen Finbar's identity.

'Elliot Dean,' he said quietly.

The boy looked as astonished as Finbar, but he quickly recovered himself and gave a sly smile.

'What are you doing here?' asked Finbar.

'I'm with a robot,' said the boy. 'And you?'

Finbar said grudgingly, 'Same here.'

'Are you going to appear on the show?' the boy asked.

Finbar shook his head.

'I thought not.' The boy gave his sly smile again.

'I suppose you are,' said Finbar, knowing how the boy had

enjoyed the rounds of parties and gallery openings while pretending to be him.

'Wag doesn't need any help from me,' said the boy. 'He's a natural performer.'

'Wag? That giant is yours?'

'In a manner of speaking.' The boy glanced in a mirror and straightened the jacket of his lime green suit. 'Must hurry. Good luck, Finbar!'

'Hang on!' said Finbar. 'You're Dean! Hester mentioned you.'

'That's right,' said the boy.

'What do you mean, "that's right"?' said Finbar. 'Are you called Dean or Elliot?'

The boy made a face. 'Dean Elliot's my name.'

'Then why did you tell me . . . ?'

'Don't know,' said the boy. 'You asked me my name when we talked on the gobetween. I could see it was important to you and I really wanted to tell you the truth. I don't know why I switched the names. I've got to go.'

Finbar stood in the doorway to let him pass, feeling churned up inside. When they last met on the gobetween he had told Elliot – or rather, Dean – that he had no bad feelings towards him. This had been true at the time, but it was a different matter seeing him swagger down the corridor after admitting to lying. What was Dean doing with a robot like Wag? Had he stolen him?

'Two minutes,' said the loud voice.

As Finbar slipped into his seat, he noticed his mother in the centre row and thought how happy she looked. He caught her eye and she blew him a kiss. She nudged Gavin and Ju who looked across and waved.

'Welcome to *Robot Einstein*!' Rick Rhodes seemed to have sprung from nowhere on to the studio floor. 'Let's meet our judges . . .'

Finbar looked across at the panel as the presenter made his introductions. Mrs Newton, the show's psychologist, was almost unrecognizable in her crimson dress and fluffy hairstyle. Dr Boris Lom, the Head of Robotics at LifeCorp, was a handsome man with an easy smile. Ken Young, the social scientist, had a stern expression as if he was constantly thinking.

Rick Rhodes addressed the audience. 'You may not have clapped a robot before, but these are no ordinary robots, remember! So let's give a big hand for our first contestant, Olga!'

The silver robot glided across the floor and took his hand in hers. 'Hello Rick,' she said in her husky voice. 'I am so pleased to meet you.'

Although he had interviewed many would-be Robot Einsteins, Rick Rhodes seemed taken aback by her greeting. 'The pleasure's mine,' he spluttered. 'Now, tell me Olga, what are your strengths?'

'I care about people,' said the robot.

* * *

In the green room, Eager watched the show on the gobetween. His concentration was broken by Wag, who kept asking questions that he answered himself. 'Where do robots live? Tin Can Alley!'

Hester came in, carrying a lexiscreen that she handed to Eager. 'Here are some problems to test your computational power . . . Do as many as you can.'

She left and Eager settled down to answer the questions. There seemed to be a lot of them. He couldn't help glancing at the show. Olga was looking at Rick Rhodes with an expression of deep sympathy. 'Why aren't you married, Rick?'

'Well, er . . . one of these days,' stammered the presenter.

'It must be difficult for you,' said Olga.

Rick Rhodes seemed to know what 'it' was, for he lowered his eyes and said, 'Yes it is, Olga. The pressure of my job, fame, travel . . .'

'Yes, yes,' said Olga soothingly.

Eager set about question one. It was an easy enough calculation. But the numbers involved in the questions grew increasingly large and without using a gobetween he couldn't answer them. Unlike robots with immense computing power, he was no cleverer than a human when it came to big numbers.

In the studio, Rick Rhodes was saying, 'And here they are! The husband and wife team who built Olga.'

There was a round of applause as the couple came on to the floor.

'Now you're both technocrats—'

'I'm a biochemist,' the woman corrected him. 'We pooled our talents to create Olga. We wanted a robot that really understands emotions. So we built a robot that could feel emotions herself.'

Hester had re-entered the green room and overheard the last remark. 'Oh no, another tricky one,' she groaned.

'What do you mean?' asked Eager.

She shot him a look. 'No one likes to talk about robots with emotions because the Ban made them illegal. Now that LifeCorp is looking for robots like Olga, we're having to admit that they exist after all.'

Eager thought, not for the first time, that the human world was very complicated.

'Why are emotions so important to LifeCorp?' he asked.

'If a robot is really going to understand people, it has to understand emotions,' said Hester. 'Try as we might, we're never free of our feelings. Imagine how hard it is for someone who doesn't recognize anger or fear or sadness in others . . .' She broke off. 'What am I saying? You're a robot. You can't imagine things the way we do.'

Before Eager could correct her, a burst of applause drew

their attention back to the screen. 'The judges are praising Olga,' she said.

'Olga seems very sympathetic,' said Eager.

Hester nodded. 'She does, doesn't she? Perhaps she's the super-advanced robot that everyone's hoping for.' She bent down to take Eager's lexiscreen and left the room.

The red-haired animat returned. 'Wag, you're on.'

twenty-five

Finbar had spotted Dean Elliot, at the end of the row. He was careful to avoid eye contact. But when the huge robot appeared he couldn't resist a glance. Dean was sitting perfectly still, a smug smile on his face.

Rick Rhodes called, 'Come on over, Wag.'

The giant robot lumbered across the floor. 'Hello Rick. Are you OK? Why have you got a jelly in one ear and a sponge cake in the other?'

'I beg your pardon?'

'Oh, you're a trifle deaf!' said Wag.

Rick Rhodes waited for the audience to stop laughing. 'Very funny, Wag. Why did they call you Wag, by the way?'

'I'm a World Amusement Generator,' said the robot.

'So you generate jokes. I guessed as much,' said Rick Rhodes. 'But tell us, why "world"?'

'I can tell jokes in every language.' The robot said two syllables that sounded very similar.

'Was that funny?' asked Rick Rhodes.

'It was, in Japanese.'

More laughter greeted this.

'How do you get on with your Japanese in Japan?' asked the presenter.

'I have no problems at all, Rick. But the Japanese do!'

Even Rick Rhodes laughed this time. 'So you like travelling, Wag.'

'Oh yes,' said the robot. 'I went to France last year. I saw the plastic box that runs around Paris . . .'

'The what?'

'You know, the lunch-pack of Notre Dame.'

'I think you mean hunch-back,' said the presenter.

'I'd never have noticed, Rick. You've got a good tailor,' said Wag.

Roars of laughter came from the audience as the robot kept up a string of jokes. Finbar took a quick look at Dean Elliot and saw that he was grinning from ear to ear.

Eventually Rick Rhodes could no longer keep a straight face. 'You are a wag, aren't you? Let's hear from the judges. I hope it isn't curtains for you, Wag.'

'Don't worry,' said the robot, 'I'll pull myself together!'

Boris Lom was the first judge to speak. 'Well, you can't help but like him, can you? There aren't many robots I'd invite to dinner, but I'd make an exception for Wag.'

'Let's hear from the psychologist,' said Rick Rhodes. 'Lily?'

Lily Newton was still chuckling. 'Humour is a neglected area of intelligence, Rick. But look how much we depend on it. We choose our friends because they share our sense of humour; we joke to break the ice or cheer ourselves up; we use humour to explain things. Imagine life without laughter – it would be pretty bleak, wouldn't it?'

Ken Young said gravely, 'It's the hardest thing to programme a machine to understand humour. Humour isn't about what *is*, it's about what *isn't*. We laugh because it shows things differently to how we expect them to be. If you don't understand the world, you don't get the joke.' He shook his head. 'How the manufacturers got Wag to understand all this, I'll never know. I take my hat off to them.'

'Well,' said Rick Rhodes, 'we have with us tonight a young representative of the technocrats who built Wag . . .' He gestured to Dean Elliot who gave a slight bow as the audience clapped.

Finbar clenched his fists. He only relaxed them when Eager came through the studio door.

twenty-six

Eager had been too busy recalling what he knew about philosophy to pay much attention to Wag. He did notice that there was a lot of laughter. He thought the audience must be very friendly. He gave them a wave as he entered the studio.

'Our final contestant tonight is Eager,' said Rick Rhodes. 'I'm eager to meet you, Eager, and I hope you're eager to be on the show.'

The robot looked at him in dismay as he remembered the unfortunate conversation with Olga.

Rick Rhodes coughed. 'One wag is probably enough for tonight.'

The audience tittered.

'You're rather more serious, aren't you, Eager? I gather you're interested in philosophy,' continued the presenter.

'Yes,' said Eager. 'I'm interested in how to live my life. When you ask questions about the world you see the wonder of it . . .'

'How thought-provoking,' said the presenter. 'Well, our judges have prepared some philosophical questions for you. Boris?'

The judge clasped his hands together. 'This is a centuries-old question, Eager. Are you ready? How many angels can fit on a pinhead?'

Eager stared at Boris. Was he all right? He looked normal enough, and Eager could see that the other judges were waiting attentively for a response. The question must be a serious one, after all. The robot tilted his head to increase the thinking power to his brain.

He considered what he knew about angels. Some of the paintings he had seen showed them as enormous beings, larger than humans. On the other hand, if the artists had never seen real angels, who could say they were not minuscule, like the cilia on Jonquil's fibres? What if angels were as small as nanobots, or even atoms?

As for a pinhead (which Eager understood to be the flat top of a pin used in sewing), it was small, but easily observable by a human eye. Therefore, it was possible that a large number of angels could sit on a pinhead. Their wings posed a problem, but perhaps they folded them back . . .

'Excuse me, Dr Lom,' he said. 'Did you say "sit" or "fit"?'

For some reason, the audience laughed. Boris Lom looked bemused. 'I said "fit".'

Ju sat in the audience, willing Eager to succeed. She noticed that Finbar was frowning at the robot. She tried to catch his eye and failed.

'One more minute,' said Rick Rhodes.

Eager tilted his head again. Of course, there was something he had overlooked. 'Excuse me, Dr Lom . . .'

'Yes?'

'When you say angels, are you thinking of cherubs?'

There was a ripple of laughter.

Dr Lom said testily, 'No, I wasn't thinking of cherubs.'

'That's good. Cherubs are quite plump,' said Eager.

The audience burst into applause.

Lily Newton called, 'We're waiting for your answer, Eager.'

'I have it!' he cried. 'Thousands or even millions of angels might fit on the pinhead. Though I think they'd better stand on tiptoe. But no one can say the exact number.'

'Why not?' asked Rick Rhodes.

'Because we can't see them, of course,' said Eager.

Dr Lom leant forward. 'Then how do we know they are there?'

Eager asked, 'How do you know you have atoms in your body?'

The technocrat looked taken aback. 'My fellow scientists tell me they are there.'

'So you believe they are there?' said Eager.

'Certainly,' said Dr Lom.

'Has anyone seen them?' asked Eager.

'Well, not with their eyes,' said Dr Lom. 'But scientists have measured and weighed them . . .'

'Are they as fat as cherubs?' asked Mrs Newton.

The audience laughed.

Dr Lom gave a fleeting smile. 'We may not be able to see atoms, but machines can detect and create an image of them,' he said.

'Perhaps we need a machine to detect angels, before we say whether they are there or not,' retorted Eager.

The audience clapped loudly. Ju found that her jaw ached and realized it was due to the release of tension.

'Thank you very much, Eager,' said Rick Rhodes. 'Could you explain your reasoning?'

The robot talked about paintings and nanobots, but the audience kept interrupting him with more clapping and laughter. He remembered they had laughed a lot at Wag, too. Perhaps the bright lights were making them dizzy-headed. He began to feel cross.

'I've seen that expression on his face before,' whispered Gavin to Marcia. 'Eager takes his philosophy very seriously.'

Rick Rhodes turned to the judges. 'What do you think, Lily?'

Lily Newton beamed. 'He's a bit of a wag, too, isn't he?'

The audience clapped in agreement. She added, 'I'm impressed by the logic of his argument too, as far as it goes.'

'Which is quite far enough for me,' said Ken Young, to further gales of laughter.

Eager rounded on Rick Rhodes. 'Is that it? I was looking forward to discussing the purpose of life.'

'That's a tall order,' said the presenter.

'I hope to find my own purpose in life, at least,' said Eager.

Someone from the back row shouted, 'What about comedy?'

Eager shot him a look.

Rick Rhodes said quickly, 'Well, everyone, you've met all our contestants for tonight. It's over to the judges for their verdict. Who is tonight's Robot Einstein?'

Eager sat down beside Finbar, glad his moment of fame was over. He scarcely heard the judges as they discussed the robots. Words such as emotional intelligence, cognitive ability, and meta-cognition drifted over him.

Eventually Rick Rhodes stepped forward. 'Ready everyone? Tonight's Robot Einstein is – Wag!'

From the corner of his eye, Finbar saw Dean Elliot leap from his seat and punch the air. Finbar stood up and quickly shepherded Eager out of the studio.

twenty-seven

Outside, Gavin was waiting by his hovercar to take everyone home. He and Marcia hadn't seen Eager since his return to the Bell family and they greeted him warmly.

'Well done, I'm proud of you,' said Gavin.

'You should have won,' said Marcia. 'That Wag is nothing but a joke machine, and a bad one at that.' She put her arm around her son. 'Don't you agree, Finbar?'

Finbar muttered his agreement.

'Let's go out for a meal to celebrate Eager taking part,' said Gavin.

Ju hung back with Finbar. 'Are you OK? You look pale.'

'I'm fine,' said Finbar, getting into the hovercar.

Ju thought he must be disappointed that Eager had lost. She had just climbed in after him when a shout rang out.

'Miss Morris! Excuse me!' A figure ran down the street towards them. Behind him, the studio was a bright oasis in the night. Dr Lom arrived breathless at the hovercar. 'How do you do, Miss Morris? I understand Eager is your son's robot.'

Marcia said charmingly, 'We prefer to think Eager is his own robot.'

'An interesting view,' said Dr Lom. 'We were struck by his—'

'Anything you have to say about Eager, you can address to him,' said Marcia.

'Of course,' said Dr Lom, turning to the robot. 'There could only be one winner tonight, Eager. But the judges were very impressed by you and Olga. We'd like you to come and work with us, as well as Wag.'

Inside the car, Ju and Finbar exchanged surprised glances.

'I entered the competition because I wanted to help,' said Eager. 'I've no reason to change my mind.'

'In that case,' said Dr Lom, 'can I take you to LifeCorp tonight? Olga and Wag are about to go there too.'

Eager hesitated. He was looking forward to hearing Gavin and Marcia's news. But he could see Olga and Wag waiting by a flying pod and was curious to know what they would be doing. 'I should like to start my new job now,' he said.

'Then you must go,' said Gavin. 'But there was something I wanted to ask you. Can you wait five minutes, Dr Lom?'

The doctor nodded. He looked mystified as Gavin and the robot stood under a streetlamp, talking.

Marcia said, 'I don't suppose you "ask" robots in your job, Dr Lom?'

'Er, no,' he replied. 'We program them and tell them what to do. But I can understand that with a robot as intelligent as Eager it may feel more comfortable to address him as a friend.'

Marcia smiled. 'You could say that.'

Gavin and Eager had finished their conversation. The robot said goodbye and followed Dr Lom to the flying pod.

Ju called out, 'Finbar and I will come and visit you soon!'

twenty-eight

Eager was pleased to find that Hester was travelling with them. She sat opposite the robots, clutching a lexiscreen. 'Dr Lom has persuaded me to come and work for LifeCorp, since I get on well with you robots,' she explained.

Eager looked round at Wag and Olga but they wore distant expressions. He guessed they had lowered their power to rest. He turned to the window. Below was a galaxy of white lights. They crossed the city and the lights thinned out. A huge glass building rose in the dark, like a ship at sea. This was LifeCorp's headquarters. Eager had been there before.

The flying pod was over the grounds now, but instead of swooping down it flew on.

Eager grew concerned. Dr Lom had said he was taking them to LifeCorp. Seconds later the flying pod landed in front of a low building with a flat roof. Dr Lom turned in his seat. 'You can get out now. Hester will show you the way. I'll see you tomorrow.'

The young woman led the robots towards the building. A huge red and grey ball on the roof showed that it belonged to LifeCorp. But, strangely, the sign above the entrance was dimly lit and Eager couldn't read it. The reception area was in shadow too, as though no one was expecting the robots.

Hester seemed lost. She hesitated between doors, finally choosing the widest. Beyond was a huge room, the length of the building. Its blue walls shimmered as luminous sea creatures darted across them. A shiny silver carpet covered most of the hall. Again, the lighting was low.

At first Eager thought he must be in an aquarium. But as he followed Hester along a tiled path, he realized it was a swimming pool. The light-emitting sea creatures were simulations; and the silver carpet was the pool's safety cover.

Hester stopped at the far corner where tropical plants and rocks framed a sitting area. She smiled. 'This is where I leave you, with the other Robot Einsteins. I'll be back tomorrow.' She retraced her steps.

Peering over the rocks, Eager made out the shadows of three more robots. None of them was of a kind he recognized. Though he was ready to rest, Eager went over to the pool. His reflection on the silver cover stared back at him. Why were they in a swimming pool, he wondered. Was there no room for them in the main building?

A taller reflection appeared beside Eager's. 'What do you think we're here for?' said a glum voice. 'Competitive swimming?'

Eager swung round. 'Cedric!'

It was hard to believe that he had seen the BDC4 only that afternoon: so much had happened since.

'I suppose you won that robot competition,' said Cedric.

'No,' said Eager. He explained about Dr Lom's request.

'You volunteered twice? I thought you had more sense!' cried Cedric.

'Aren't you here to help too?' asked Eager.

'Certainly not. I was picked up this afternoon, just after you left me,' said the BDC4. 'There was time to run for it, but then they would have taken Orville.'

'Didn't they take it?' said Eager, although he was unsure who 'they' were.

Cedric smiled for the first time. 'It wasn't there for them to take. But they got me.'

'I'm sorry,' said Eager. 'You went there to drop me off. But who are "they", and why have they brought you here?'

'Your friends at LifeCorp, of course,' said Cedric. 'But don't apologize. Their patrols would have spotted me sooner or later. I couldn't resist going up in Orville.'

Eager tilted his head as he thought. 'If you don't want to help them, why have they brought you here?'

'Against my will, you mean?' Cedric laughed bitterly. 'No one cares what robots want or feel.'

'That's not true—' Eager began.

'Stick with your human friends, then,' said the BDC4, walking away.

Eager realized that he had been wrong to think of Cedric as his friend. He was just like the BDC4s that Eager had met before – hostile to humans and scornful of robots like him. He found a sun-lounger to sit on and turned down his power. Eventually the lights in the hall were dimmed too.

twenty-nine

The next day Ju and Finbar slept longer than usual, after a late night in the city. They met at the breakfast table. Mr and Mrs Bell had finished eating and were upstairs, getting ready for work.

'Morning,' said Finbar, with a grin.

Ju was pleased to see that he was in brighter spirits. During the meal the previous night he had hardly said a word. It surprised her that he had taken Eager's losing so badly – if that was the reason for his silence. Finbar was not the competitive type.

She helped herself to marmalade. 'I wonder what Eager's doing now.'

'He was pretty excited about going, wasn't he?' said Finbar.

Ju smiled as she remembered how the robot had hurried over to the flying pod. 'I wonder how long he'll be there. But he'll have to come home for your mum's wedding next weekend.' She chewed her toast, thoughtfully. 'Do you need new clothes for the wedding? I'll help you shop—'

'No, I don't!' stormed Finbar, pushing back his chair.

'I was only offering . . .'

He had left the room.

What did I say? thought Ju.

Later, they walked to the bus stop in silence. Ju tried to think of something to say, but one look at Finbar's cloudy face warned her to keep quiet. They had reached the top of the avenue when Finbar said, 'Listen, sorry I snapped. Do you want to know why?'

'If you like,' said Ju.

They turned the corner. Finbar lowered his voice. 'Remember when I flew here last summer, I lent my jinn to a boy on the Sorbjet? He downloaded the contents and then pretended to be me.'

'How could I forget?' said Ju. 'We saw him on the gobey, impersonating you in Amsterdam.'

Finbar went on, 'Well, he was at the show last night, with Wag.'

'The boy in the front row!' said Ju. 'I thought he looked familiar when the light was on him. He's changed a lot.'

'Looks older, and less pasty-faced,' said Finbar. 'But his dress sense is just as weird. Remember, he used my account to buy clothes – those shiny coloured suits?'

Ju sighed. 'So that's why you lost your temper with me – because I mentioned new clothes.'

'I don't understand it,' said Finbar. 'I wasn't angry last time we met.'

'You met him again?' Ju exclaimed.

Finbar looked sheepish. 'On the gobey. Jonquil connected me to the gallery and he was there. I told him I didn't mind if he impersonated me. But he stopped soon after.'

The hoverbus homed in on the bus stop.

'You never told me,' said Ju.

'I didn't get a chance to,' said Finbar. 'And I wanted to forget about it.'

'Are you climbing aboard or not?' asked the animat-conductor.

They stepped into the hoverbus.

'I wonder where he got that robot,' said Ju, as they sat down.

'That's what I've been thinking,' said Finbar. 'I wouldn't put anything past Dean Elliot.'

'Is that his name?'

'Apparently. I asked his name on the gobey and he told me Elliot Dean. I found out the truth last night. Though I still didn't know which to believe.' Finbar gave a sheepish smile. 'I think I'm so cross with him because I expected him to have changed. I've been busy forgiving him and he acted like he couldn't care less.'

Ju said, 'You know, we might meet him again at LifeCorp if we go to visit Eager.'

'If we do I won't lose my temper,' said Finbar. 'Promise.'

Ju raised her eyebrows. 'Well, I might, if I hear another of Wag's jokes.'

Finbar laughed for a long time, as if to demonstrate that Ju's jokes were a lot funnier than the robot's.

thirty

The lights in the room became bright. Eager stood up from the sun-lounger. Olga and Wag were standing beside the pool, and the other robots were beginning to stir. Eager looked at them with interest. Two were identical, built like insects. One, a large spherical head on a squat body, looked familiar. It walked up to Eager. 'High pressure, low visibility,' it said, in a male voice.

'I beg your pardon?' said Eager.

'Misty.'

'Hello, Misty. I'm Eager.'

'The *weather* is misty,' said the robot. 'My name is Wilf. International Weather Forecaster. Shall I tell you today's forecast?'

'I don't mind "weather" you do!' said Wag, who had come up to them.

'More snow . . .' said Wilf.

'Why is it snowing in summer?' asked Eager.

A voice behind him said, 'You're wasting your time

with these machines, Eager. None of them can see beyond his own nose.'

Eager turned to Cedric. 'Everyone is very friendly.'

'I thought *I* was your friend,' said Cedric.

Eager was at a loss what to say. Cedric's head drooped. It was a strange pose for such a proud-looking robot. 'I'm not used to having friends,' Cedric continued. 'It's not surprising I don't know how to keep one.'

'I haven't stopped being your friend!' cried Eager. 'But you—'

'Good morning, everyone. Lovely day for a dip.' Dr Lom, dressed in a grey suit, was striding along the poolside. Eager hurried to greet him, and regretted his keenness. He didn't want the man to think he was volunteering for a swim.

'Good morning, Dr Lom,' said Olga. 'How are you feeling today?'

'Very well, thank you Olga. Good morning, Wag. How are you?'

The giant robot lumbered over. 'I'm fine, Doctor. Except I keep seeing yellow and green spots before my eyes.'

Dr Lom looked anxious. 'Have you seen a technocrat?'

'No, Doctor, just yellow and green spots.'

'Ha, ha! Very good,' said the man. He made a note with a stylus on his lexiscreen. 'Good morning, Wilf. Shall I need my umbrella today?'

'No, Dr Lom. But I hope you've remembered your thermal conductivity underwear.'

'I have indeed,' said Dr Lom.

The insects scuttled towards him in tandem, tap-tapping against the tiled floor.

'Good morning, Bug and Doug. And here's Eager, our philosopher.' He turned to Cedric. 'And you are? I'm afraid I don't know your name. You arrived yesterday?'

'That's right,' said Cedric.

'And your name is?'

'Brad,' lied Cedric.

'Brad. A common name for a BDC4, but I'll look you up in our records.' He sat on a rock. 'Gather round, please.'

'Who does he think he is?' whispered Cedric.

Eager looked quizzically at him.

'Here's Eager, our philosopher,' mimicked Cedric. 'Has a human ever been that attentive to you before?'

'Hurry up!' called Dr Lom. He looked very satisfied as the robots formed a semicircle around him. The insects settled at his feet. 'What a fine team you are. The fruits of twenty years' top-class scientific research.'

'Heaven help us,' muttered Cedric.

Dr Lom frowned at him. 'You're here because we need your help. As you know, our robots and computers run this planet. Almost everything depends on LifeCorp. We have rivals, of course, but even they have to design their systems to be compatible with ours.'

He tapped his fingers together. 'However, we have problems. The most pressing is the dramatic change in our weather patterns. We need better technology to help us understand what is happening to the water cycle. Unfortunately, our existing machines are developing faults, as all machines do over time—'

Cedric interrupted. 'Can't you repair them?'

'We don't know how,' said Dr Lom. 'The technology was developed decades ago. Even the animats are ten years old. Unfortunately, we no longer have the expertise to fix things, or to build something new.'

'Greed,' said Cedric, shaking his domed head. 'You wanted to save money so you haven't trained enough technocrats.'

'We might have underestimated the need,' said Dr Lom. 'But the Ban put off many people from becoming scientists.'

'Can't you train new ones?' said Cedric. 'There must be some scientists left who understand the technology.'

Dr Lom sighed. 'There are. For example, Professor Ogden who helped design you BDC4s and the animats . . .'

The mention of Professor Ogden left Eager's system confused. The doctor's tone suggested that the professor was a friend of LifeCorp, but Eager knew he had resigned from the company not once, but twice.

Dr Lom went on, 'But such men are growing old and there aren't enough of them. Nor is there time for them to train new technocrats. That's why we need you.'

Eager recovered himself. 'What for?' he asked.

'First of all, to build us an army of fault-finding machines – intelligent robots that can spot and repair the mistakes . . .' said Dr Lom.

Eager thought, That's what Jonquil is doing! Had Professor Ogden known of the problems all along? Was that why he built Allegra and asked her to create Jonquil? Why was he keeping them secret from LifeCorp . . . ?

'And secondly, to work out what's happening with the weather,' continued Dr Lom.

'What makes you think we can do all that?' Cedric asked.

Dr Lom paused. 'We've chosen you because you appear to understand our world. And because you're robots, you have computational skills that we lack. Perhaps you can find the solutions we can't.'

'That might be true of these robots,' said Cedric, nodding at Wag and the others, 'but I'm an ordinary BDC4. LifeCorp built me and programmed me just like any other robot.'

The man raised an eyebrow. 'None of your fellow BDC4s has been known to take a jaunt in a homemade flying machine – which we've yet to find, by the way. And you're arguing with me now in a very human manner.'

Cedric looked away. The man stood up. 'I shall leave you now. Hester will come soon with some questions to test your general knowledge and common-sense understanding of the world. Tomorrow we'll see how you work together.'

'Don't worry, Dr Lom. We shall do our best,' said Olga.

thirty-one

As Dr Lom left the hall, Wag said, 'Did you hear about the scientist who mixed a four-leaf clover with stinging nettles?'

'No,' said Eager.

'He had a rash of good luck,' said Wag.

It took Eager a moment to see the joke. He laughed.

Cedric said, 'I've got a better one. Did you hear about the scientists who were afraid machines would go wrong? Well, they did. Ha, ha, ha.'

The other robots stared at him.

'You seem to find that amusing,' drawled Olga.

Cedric sat down on the rock that Dr Lom had vacated. 'People have always been scared that robots will go wrong. They imagine us turning evil and threatening them. But robots are going wrong simply because *they don't work properly*! And it's the humans' fault! Isn't that a good joke?' He started to laugh again.

Wag said, 'What goes "ha, ha," clunk?'

'I don't know,' said Eager.

'A robot laughing its head off!' said Wag.

Olga said, 'I think laughter is the best medicine.'

Cedric raised his eyebrows.

'What is going to happen now?' asked Eager.

'You heard the doctor,' said Cedric. 'Machines are going wrong. Everything's linked by the gobetween these days, so my guess is one thing will lead to another. No wonder they can't solve the weather problem. We're lucky the hovertrains are still running.'

'You mean, everything will stop?' said Eager.

Cedric said, 'Who can say? Dr Lom looked desperate to me. They must be desperate to want our help.'

'We are the fruit of years of scientific research,' said Olga.

Cedric shook his head. He took Eager by the arm and led him under a palm tree. He said quietly, 'Tell me Eager, how many *Robot Einstein* shows are happening across the world?'

Eager looked blank.

'Twenty?' suggested Cedric. 'Let's say half of the winners can truly think for themselves. So, with you and me, that makes a dozen self-aware robots in the world. And we're supposed to solve the weather problem!'

Eager said, 'What about Olga and Wag and Wilf . . . ?'

'Those zombies? They're no better than animats,' said Cedric. 'They just respond to triggers. There's nothing going on inside.'

'I can't believe that!' cried Eager. 'And they were chosen by the judges.'

'The judges don't believe in self-aware machines,' said Cedric. 'They're just hoping to find some brighter than average robots. Well, perhaps these will do the job. But I don't want to hang around and find out. I didn't like the way Dr Lom looked at me . . . If he suspects my secret, I'm done for.'

'Your secret?' said Eager.

Cedric whispered, 'Haven't you guessed? I was never returned to the factory with the other BDC4s to be reprogrammed. I—'

Hester's arrival interrupted them. Two animats in grey overalls accompanied her, each carrying several gobetweens. Hester called, 'Hello, everyone.' She no longer wore the dark clothes that the staff at the studio dressed in. She was sporting a red jumpsuit, topped by a short grey cape.

'Good morning, Hester,' chorused Wilf and Olga.

'What sits in a fruit tree calling for help?' asked Wag.

'I don't know,' said the young woman.

'A damson in distress!'

Hester smiled. 'Well, that's me,' she said, settling herself on a rock. 'Fortunately, you can help.' She looked at Cedric and Eager. 'I'd like to know your special skills. Let me give you some examples . . .' She pointed to the robots as she spoke. 'Doug and Bug are experts at covering different terrains, and can perform microscopic repair operations. Wilf is a weather forecaster – we have high hopes that he can unravel the problem with the water cycle. Wag is a keen observer of human foibles, and Olga has deep emotional understanding.'

'The world's gone mad,' murmured Cedric. 'I knew I should have stayed at home.'

'I shall be recording your answers on my lexiscreen,' said Hester. 'Eager, I know you're interested in philosophy. Do you have a special skill?'

Eager had been trying to think. 'The Bells like my pancakes. But I know you're not interested in that.'

'Not really,' said Hester sadly. 'Anything else?'

Eager had no unique robot talents, unlike Allegra and Jonquil. 'I can lengthen my arms and legs.'

Hester brightened up. 'That could be useful. What about you, Brad?'

Cedric said, 'I'm very good at sweeping leaves.'

'Sweeping leaves?'

'Oh yes,' said Cedric. 'No garden vacubot could do a better job.'

'Why bother?' asked Hester. 'A vacubot sucks up the leaves perfectly.'

'That's the problem. Where is the artistry in that?' said Cedric.

'Artistry?'

Cedric hissed to Eager, 'Wish she'd stop repeating

everything.' Aloud he said, 'Unlike a vacubot, I never clear the garden completely. I like to see a few leaves scattered around. It's more natural.'

'It is, isn't it?' cried Hester. 'Nature isn't neat and tidy. It's sort of loose around the edges.'

'I couldn't have put it better myself,' said Cedric, deadpan.

Hester smiled. 'Well, I'll leave you to do your tests. There's a gobetween for each of you. I'll see you again tomorrow.'

thirty-two

Eager was longing to turn down his power. All day the gobetween had bombarded him with questions. What is the equator? Where does celery come from? What do people like for breakfast in the western hemisphere? Use the following words in sentences: guarantee, slippery, dual, popular . . .

His system was in a spin and he was grateful when the lights dimmed at last. He noticed that Wag and Olga didn't chatter as usual as they settled for the night. Eager began to process his thoughts.

An hour or so passed. The sound of footsteps disturbed him. He looked towards the pool and was startled to see two pairs of dancing red lights. He realized they must be robots' eyes, but why were they moving so strangely? He felt the touch of metal on his arm. 'Animats with night vision,' hissed Cedric. 'Now's our chance to escape. Come with me!'

Before Eager could reply, Hester's voice cried, 'What on earth are you doing?' Cedric and Eager jumped apart, guiltily.

But she was addresssing the animats. Her voice had carried in the empty hall.

A sudden blaze of light illuminated the room. The grey-clad animats were stumbling towards the pool, their arms around a long black parcel. Whatever was inside was thrashing about, and they struggled to keep hold of it. Eager felt panic. Were the animats about to drown someone? He had time to notice the source of the light, before Hester shouted, 'Wilf, turn off your beam! Go back to the rocks.'

It was dark again.

Cedric whispered, 'Perhaps they're setting up tomorrow's test. I knew there was a reason to bring us to a swimming pool.'

'But whatever it is is alive!' said Eager.

There was a huge splash. Hester shrieked, 'I'm soaked! Animats, get out of here!'

Footsteps ran towards the door, and there was silence. Eager walked carefully to the edge of the pool. The silver cover had gone and he was looking down on a deep blackness. 'Wilf, will you turn on your light again?' he called.

The robot shone a beam on to the water. 'Choppy,' he said. 'Shipping alert three.'

Something or someone was furiously churning the water in the middle of the pool. Eager was about to jump to the rescue when he felt Cedric's restraining hand. 'I think you'll find it can swim,' he said, in a curious tone.

Eager remembered that this was more than he could do.

A dusky shape leapt into the air. Eager had a glimpse of long dark hair and a slim metal torso, before the figure plunged into the pool again. 'It's an animat!' he cried.

Seconds later, water parted at the opposite end. Wilf swung his beam round. There was a glint of silver as something dived in. For a second, a silver-grey tail stood proud of the water.

Wilf said matter-of-factly, 'It's a fish.'

thirty-three

Thrown into darkness once more, Eager spent a restless night. He couldn't stop thinking about the new arrivals. Although he had heard only one splash, there were at least two of them – the slender, long-haired animat and the fish. How many other entities had been slipped into the pool? Who were they?

Now and then water lapped against the poolside, but the churning had stopped. At last the lights came on. The gobetween announced a set of questions for the day. The other robots sat among the rocks, facing the screens.

Eager looked across at Cedric, who beckoned to him. 'Time to meet our mysterious visitor,' said the BDC4. Visitor? Eager was about to correct him, but Cedric had hurried to the side of the pool. He called softly, 'Hello! Hello!'

Standing beside him, Eager saw a dart of silver-grey under the water. It was the fish. But the head and shoulders that appeared were those of a female animat! Eager wondered where the fish had gone.

Cedric knelt down. 'Who are you?' he asked.

The animat stared at him. Eager saw that her eyes were green and her skin had a pale blue tinge. She was the most beautiful entity he had ever seen. 'Who's asking?' The tone was brusque, but her voice was like honey.

'I'm Cedric, and this is Eager. I'm a reluctant guest of LifeCorp, as I imagine you are.'

The robot relaxed her stare. 'My name is Dulcie.'

Dulcie. Eager had an image of the stream tripping over stones in the wood.

'I'm called after a seaweed,' Dulcie said. 'My hair resembles dulse, which grows in the Atlantic. It acts as camouflage when I come to the surface.'

Cedric said gallantly, 'Seaweed is the common term. I prefer sea vegetable, or algae, don't you?'

Dulcie gave him a cold look. 'I don't care what you call it. I've been given humans' language, but I prefer to speak sea tongue.'

Cedric leant closer. 'Who built you, Dulcie?'

She gave a fleeting smile. 'Wouldn't you like to know? I bet you can't guess what I am.'

'I know what you are,' said Cedric. 'You're a mermaid.'

Eager shot him a look. A mermaid! So there wasn't a fish in the pool, after all! Only Dulcie. But like the Greek gods, mermaids belonged to myths . . .

'My creators had a sense of humour, if you can call it that,' said Dulcie.

'You don't seem very fond of them,' said Cedric.

Dulcie tossed back her purple-black hair. 'I hate humans,' she said. 'In fact, I don't care for many of the larger mammals. Except for dolphins, of course. Oh, and humpback whales. They're very courteous.'

Eager was dumbfounded. Hate humans? He thought of his friends – the Bells, Professor Ogden. Surely Dulcie would not hate them, if ever they met?

'Why do you hate humans?' he asked.

She jumped in the air, revealing her smooth tail. It slapped against the water as she landed. 'Nasty, greedy, two-timing creatures,' she said. 'I'd rather deal with a shark any day. Humans tricked me into coming here.'

The mermaid went on, 'They've been after me for weeks. Once, they were waiting with a hidden cage. My friends, the dolphins, warned me it was a trap.'

'But they caught you in the end,' said Cedric.

She grimaced. 'I made a foolish mistake.'

'You're not the only one,' said Cedric.

'Good morning, everyone!' boomed a voice behind him.

Dulcie dived and disappeared.

Dr Lom came to the poolside. 'I see you've met our new friend. Somewhat shy,' he said.

Cedric stood up. He towered over the doctor. 'Why is she here?' he asked. 'She's a mermaid.'

'Yes!' Dr Lom laughed. 'There was a discussion as to whether she should be made a diver or a fish. Some clever bod said, "Why not make her both?" Though as you will have noticed, her tail is smooth, not scaly. She is part whale, not fish.'

Cedric said thoughtfully, 'So you built her to be a deep-sea diver?'

Dr Lom wagged his finger teasingly. 'You've asked enough questions, Brad. You have work to do. Intelligence tests today.'

Wag called from his sun-lounger: 'Fish aren't clever.'

'Why do you say that?' asked Dr Lom.

'They're forever in schools,' said Wag.

'That's true' said Dr Lom, laughing. He made a note on his lexiscreen. 'Now, back to work.'

thirty-four

Once again Eager had a busy morning. The gobetween told him about a travelling salesman who wanted to visit twenty-five towns by the shortest possible route.

'Twenty-five towns?' repeated Eager. 'I think he should stay in bed and visit the towns on the gobetween.'

'Is that your answer?' said the gobetween.

Eager reflected. 'I expect his customers want to handle his products. If so, they can view them on the gobetween and wear a touch-mantle to feel them.'

'That is not an option,' said the gobetween.

Eager felt sorry for the salesman. He would have to go out, after all. All that travelling would be very tiring. Eager said, 'My friend, Gavin, travels a lot and he sometimes stays with relatives. I expect the salesman has a great-aunt in one of the towns. He should stay with her and travel to the other places from there. His great-aunt would enjoy that.'

Eager was pleased with his answer. He put down the

gobetween and looked around. The other robots were still poring over a screen. He walked to the edge of the pool, hoping for a glimpse of Dulcie. There was no sign of her, not even a ripple.

Back at the rocks, he noticed the insects crawling from under the palm trees. Eager was curious about Bug and Doug. They might look like insects, but who could tell what intelligence they possessed? Eager knew not to judge a robot by appearance. After all, Jonquil had been compared to a Christmas bauble.

The insects scurried towards Eager, vying with each other to reach him first. The winner put a leg on Eager's foot. Eager took this to be a greeting. 'How do you do?' he said. 'I'm Eager.'

The second robot circled Eager's other foot.

'Where are you from?' asked Eager.

The insects let out a squeak. Raising their front legs they began to clash against each other.

'I don't understand,' said Eager, wondering whether the squeak could be understood by a different auditory system.

'They probably don't speak to conserve energy,' said Cedric's voice. The BDC4 had a habit of appearing suddenly. 'I expect they understand, though. Doug, Bug, go back to your shelter.'

The insects stopped their sparring and scuttled behind a rock.

Eager protested, 'I was getting to know them!'

Cedric looked sadly at him. 'Why don't you want to get to know me?'

'I do,' said Eager. 'But you're angry because I want to help LifeCorp.'

'I am,' said Cedric, 'because LifeCorp doesn't deserve our help. Even if you solve their problems, do you think you'll get any credit?' He gave his bitter laugh. 'It'll be back into hiding for you, or worse.'

Eager didn't want to get into an argument with the robot. He remembered their conversation the day before. 'Cedric, why weren't you reprogrammed?'

Cedric hesitated. 'There was no need.'

'Didn't you have a dead person's memories, like the other BDC4s?' asked Eager.

Cedric gave a hollow laugh. 'Oh yes, I had a man's memories all right. But memories weren't the problem. It was passion that drove the BDC4s to disobey. They remembered the things they had enjoyed most – dancing, chatting to friends, building model flying pods. Whatever their passion, they wanted to recreate it.'

Eager asked, with interest, 'What was your passion?'

Cedric looked away. 'I had none. That's why there was no need to reprogram me.'

There was a pause. 'The man whose memories you had must have led a gloomy life,' said Eager.

'He did,' said Cedric. 'Or rather, I did, since I still have the memories. To say it was a dull life is an understatement.' He sat down on a rock. 'I lived alone, in a nice enough house, with a small garden. My neighbours said hello to me in the street, and I had a domestic robot. He was company, though he didn't have much conversation.

'I went every day to an office. Machines did most of the work. We humans were supposed to come up with bright ideas of what to do next. Somehow, it never turned out like that. Perhaps our ideas were never bright enough.

'One evening, I was walking home when I was knocked down and killed by a hoverbus.' Cedric frowned. 'Come to think of it, that was the most exciting thing that ever happened to me.'

Eager waited for him to continue, but the robot seemed lost in thought. 'A friend of mine was knocked down by a lorry,' Eager said. 'He was destroyed. He was a robot.'

'I bet they didn't recycle him as a human!' said Cedric dryly. 'Whereas, my brain patterns were transferred to a robot. I became a BDC4. It was a second chance. I vowed never again to live on the sidelines of life. I was lucky – my new owner was a scientist and I helped him in his work. I discovered skills I never knew I had.'

Cedric's voice rose. 'When LifeCorp began sending the BDC4s back to the factory, I got ready to go. My owner stopped me. He said I had never behaved threateningly and that he trusted me as his friend.' The robot shook his head as if in disbelief. 'I had never had a friend before.'

'So you stayed with your owner?' said Eager.

'Yes. If anyone asked, we said I'd been declared safe. That was true – my owner declared it! It wasn't the result of reprogramming,' said Cedric.

Eager recalled the BDC4s. He had always thought of them as robots with borrowed memories. Now he saw them differently: as humans who had been given a second chance of life. He felt sad. 'No wonder you're worried that Dr Lom will guess your secret,' he said.

Cedric gripped Eager's arm with his slender metal fingers. 'If Dr Lom has me reprogrammed it will be a second death. That's why I'm determined to escape. Come with me, Eager. What help can we give, in any case? A motley crowd like us will never build these super-robots to repair the machines, let alone bring on the rain.'

Eager's system somersaulted. Should he tell Cedric about Jonquil and his work? He remembered Professor Ogden's advice about trusting others. Whatever Cedric had just said, he was still a BDC4, and BDC4s were unpredictable.

'I'm going to stay, Cedric,' he said. 'Humans need help. I shall do my best for them.'

'As you wish,' said Cedric, walking away.

thirty-five

That afternoon, both Dr Lom and Hester came to the pool. They chatted and laughed as they walked towards the palm trees. Dulcie's head bobbed above the water and Hester waved to her, but the mermaid quickly dived.

'Good morning, everyone!' Dr Lom's greeting was breezier than ever. 'Gather round.' He and Hester sat side by side on a yellow sun-lounger.

Wag began a joke and Dr Lom held up a hand to silence him. 'Not yet. Wait until you hear today's exercise. Hester and I have come up with a way to test your cooperation, creativity and understanding at the same time! We're rather proud of ourselves. Hester?'

The young woman said excitedly, 'We're going to give you a theme. You must work together to produce whatever you like on that subject.'

'Whatever we like?' said Olga huskily. 'What would *you* like?'

'You decide,' said Dr Lom, waving his finger at her. 'A poem, play, picture, sculpture, piece of music, mathematical equation, *tableau vivant* . . .'

'Don't get too carried away,' said Cedric.

Dr Lom said sternly, 'I hope you're going to join in, Brad. After all, this is about cooperation.'

Hester tapped her foot impatiently. 'Shall we tell them the theme, Boris?'

'Go ahead,' said Dr Lom.

Hester faced the robots, her eyes shining with excitement. 'The theme is "Freedom".'

'Freedom?' said Olga.

'Yes,' said Hester. She added archly, 'Feel free to interpret it any way you wish.'

'It's a very smart idea of Hester's,' said Dr Lom. 'Can a robot understand freedom? That in itself is interesting. You could just recite what humans say, but by producing a piece of work you will show us what it really means to you.'

'How clever,' said Olga.

Dr Lom and Hester left. Cedric took their place on the yellow sun-lounger. 'Gather round!' he said, in imitation of Dr Lom.

'Are you going to help us?' asked Eager.

Cedric winked at him. 'An important subject like this? I should think so.'

'What does it mean to be free?' asked Olga.

Wag said, 'Did you hear about the three men who—?'

'Not three,' said Olga crossly. '*Free*.'

'Free winds,' said Wilf. 'Very important in navigation.'

'We could do a dance of the free winds,' drawled Olga.

A deep voice began to sing:

> 'I'm a free wind, are you a free wind?
> And are you a free wind too?
> If we three are free winds—'

'Not now, Wag,' said Olga.

'This is all very interesting,' said Cedric.

Eager looked at him in surprise. Only yesterday Cedric had been rude about the other robots.

Cedric went on, 'I've an idea that will involve us all and demonstrate to Dr Lom that we understand the theme.'

'It's important to please Dr Lom,' said Olga.

'Indeed it is,' said Cedric. 'Now listen . . .'

thirty-six

Eager slipped away. Although he was pleased that Cedric was joining in, he lacked enthusiasm. He sat on the rock nearest the pool, to think. Of course, there was always the chance that he might see Dulcie . . .

Eager used to believe that all humans were good. After all, who would want to cause pain and suffering? As time went by, he learnt that some people had bad intentions towards others. But he still thought that most humans meant well.

Now, in the space of a few days, he had met two robots that thought differently.

Cedric was not like other BDC4s, for he was kind and friendly – but he shared their scorn of humans. And Dulcie had said she hated them! Eager reminded himself that he wouldn't exist had it not been for humans. It was his duty to help them. But if he was *truly* self-aware, would he see things differently, like Cedric and Dulcie?

As long as he felt a deep attachment to people, perhaps he

could never be an independent robot. But did he want to be an independent robot if that meant breaking with his human friends? A whisper of a reply came to him – he would, if it meant he could enter Dulcie's world . . .

A splashing alerted him to the mermaid's presence. He started, and grabbed the rock to steady himself. Her head emerged from the surface of the pool. She tossed back her purple-black hair to reveal her pale elfin face. A droplet of water glistened on her cheek.

'Freedom?' she said. 'They've got a nerve.'

Eager said, 'I think they chose it as a test because a robot would not understand freedom unless it could think for itself.'

'The only freedom is the open sea,' said Dulcie.

Eager realized that he couldn't imagine Dulcie's world, much less enter it. How deep had she dived? How far had she travelled? To tropical beaches and arctic waters?

'I can't go to sea,' he said. 'The salt-water would be bad for my rubber, for one thing. But I love to look at it. They call Earth the "Blue Planet" because of all the water. Without it there would be no life here. That must include me, although I don't need water to survive. And this life-giving water is your element . . .'

Dulcie ducked under the surface, re-emerging with parted lips and dancing eyes. Eager was astonished. It was the first time he had seen her smile. What had he said?

'Some humans understand, they respect the sea,' she said. 'I've heard fishermen call it by name, I've watched people throw food and garlands of flowers to the waves.'

Eager was reminded of the myths he had read. Were there sea gods to receive these offerings?

As if she read his thoughts, Dulcie said, 'Porpoises are partial to garlands – eating them, that is.' Her tone changed. 'But many humans are destroying the sea. From coast to coast my friends are dying.'

'Dying!' echoed Eager. He recalled what he knew about the marine world. 'Sea creatures are killed by predators . . .' he began.

'That's life!' cried Dulcie. 'Death in the ocean is part of the cycle of life. Creatures die and give life to others; and so it goes on. When I talk of dying, I mean a cruel, unnecessary death.'

'How?' asked Eager. He felt bewildered.

Dulcie came closer. 'Humans are poisoning the water. They poison it with noise and chemicals and rubbish. But they'll regret it. They don't realize that they're poisoning themselves, too.'

She went on, 'You, a robot, understand that water is life-giving. How did humans forget? Tell me that?'

Eager looked into her emerald eyes. For an instant they seemed as deep and fluid as the ocean itself. 'I don't know,' he said. He thought about the Bells and Professor Ogden. They would not harm the sea deliberately.

'Perhaps humans do it by accident,' he said.

Dulcie said coldly, 'It's still a crime.' She tossed back her hair. 'For years my marine friends have been crying for help. But humans don't understand – or don't listen. When they learnt that I speak human, my friends begged me to be their voice . . .' She broke off, looking with startled eyes over Eager's shoulder. Eager turned his head as Dulcie sprang from the water. Arching backwards, she dived.

'Magnificent,' said Dr Lom, staring at the pool. 'That's where the future lies. Human engineering and bio-robotics.' He turned to Eager. 'Common robots like you will be obsolete.'

Eager stepped down from the rock. Dulcie had been telling him something important and Dr Lom had interrupted. He said crossly, 'Do humans poison the sea?'

'That's putting it strongly.' Dr Lom gave a nervous laugh. 'There have been unfortunate accidents in the past. But the oceans are vast – two-thirds of this planet is water. The amount of chemicals we pour away is literally – a drop in the ocean!' He laughed, boldly this time, before walking away.

Eager was left with an uncomfortable feeling. Why did he think, more and more, that people were lying to him? He stood at the edge of the pool. 'Dulcie, Dulcie,' he called softly.

The mermaid did not reappear. He went on, 'Dulcie, I believe what you say. I want to help. Tell me what to do.'

He waited for a while, then went to rejoin the other robots.

thirty-seven

Snow was falling when Ju woke up. It had become warm enough to wear a skirt, but now she turned a dress into trousers again, ready for the journey to the learning centre.

'It's closed,' said Finbar, as she sat down to breakfast.

She knew at once what he meant. 'Not the simulation generator again?'

He nodded. 'The Principal left a message this morning. It broke down yesterday, after we left.'

Mrs Bell had made hot chocolate. 'Why don't you work at home this morning and after lunch we can visit Eager?' she said, pouring them each a mugful. 'I'm not working today, but I don't mind going to LifeCorp so we can all see him.'

'Thanks, Gran,' said Ju. 'I've been wondering how he is.'

LifeCorp's headquarters were the other side of the city. The snow had left a threadbare white blanket over the cityscape. Finbar looked out of the hoverbus, trying to recognize places he knew. He glimpsed the Hotel Regency, where his mother was staying. Her studio was in the same street. He imagined her painting, and hoped her work was going well.

His thoughts turned to Dean Elliot. He would hate to bump into him again. Yet the boy had done nothing new to harm him. He's just an habitual liar, I suppose, thought Finbar. But behind the posing, who *was* Dean Elliot?

Ju nudged him. 'There it is.'

He caught sight of a huge glass and titanium structure, jutting up behind a high metal wall. It vanished as the hoverbus swooped them down to the pavement. Mrs Bell led the way to a gate in the wall. 'Mrs Bell and guests,' she said, as a sensor took a retinogram of her eye. The gate opened to let them pass.

The immensity of the building stunned Finbar. 'It's a giant battleship,' he said, observing the bow-like front. Inside was just as impressive. The vast domed ceiling reminded him of a cathedral, except the glass made it dazzlingly bright. People were milling around, dressed in red or grey suits.

Ju was glad she was wearing her flexi-clothes. They were so simple that she felt as sleek as the technocrats. 'Where do you think Eager is?' she asked her grandmother.

'I've no idea,' said Mrs Bell. 'This building is a labyrinth.'

She went up to the reception desk.

'Good afternoon, Mrs Bell,' said a smooth-faced male animat.

'We've come to see Eager, one of the contestants from *Robot Einstein*,' she said.

'Robot Einstein?' said the receptionist. 'He's dead.'

Mrs Bell was momentarily at a loss. Then she recovered herself to say, 'That must be Professor Einstein. Albert Einstein died many years ago. I'm talking about the robot competition.'

'There is no competition here,' said the receptionist.

Mrs Bell said patiently, 'I'd better speak to Dr Lom. Will you tell him I'd like to see him?'

'Certainly.'

A second later Dr Lom's voice came from the desk: 'Tell Mrs Bell I'll be right down.'

Finbar blinked. 'That was quick. How did that happen?'

Mrs Bell explained, 'The animat scanned my face . . .'

'I didn't notice,' said Finbar.

'With his eyes,' said Mrs Bell. 'Then he relayed the image to Dr Lom's secretary with an automatic request to see him.'

Dr Lom was not as fast as his communications system.

'Do you know him, Gran?' Ju asked as they waited.

'Oh yes. I work in his robotics department,' said Mrs Bell. 'But I'm a very junior member.'

A figure in a well-cut grey suit strode across the foyer and greeted Mrs Bell. 'Chloe, what can I do for you?'

'My friend Finbar would like to see Eager,' said Mrs Bell.

'Ah yes, Marcia Morris' son . . .' said Dr Lom.

'And this is my granddaughter, Ju.'

'How is Eager doing?' asked Ju.

'Very well, on the whole,' said Dr Lom. 'He seems most knowledgeable. But he isn't very good at algorithms.'

'Oh,' said Mrs Bell.

'An algorithm is a set of rules for solving a problem,' the doctor explained to Ju and Finbar. 'We gave Eager the travelling salesman problem – how to find the shortest possible route between several towns. Useful information for a salesman on the road!'

Finbar said, 'You mean, whether to go from A to B to C, or whether to go straight to C and then to B?'

'That's it.' Dr Lom smiled. 'It may not sound exciting, but it's one of the hardest problems to solve. Once you get above a few towns, the possible number of routes becomes astronomical. Only a completely quantum computer could find a precise answer.'

Ju said, 'How many towns was Eager asked about?'

'Twenty-five,' said Dr Lom.

'You just said it's impossible to find the answer for so many towns!' exclaimed Finbar.

'It is,' said Dr Lom. 'Although we keep hoping a robot will discover a new method to solve the problem quickly. Meanwhile, we settle for the best approximate answer.'

‘What was Eager’s best approximate answer?’ asked Ju, excitedly.

Dr Lom frowned. ‘He suggested the salesman stay with an elderly relative and go on day trips.’

Finbar and Ju burst out laughing.

‘That sounds like Eager,’ said Mrs Bell. ‘He’s very practical.’

‘Can we see him now?’ asked Ju.

‘I’m afraid not,’ said the man. ‘The robots are devising a performance piece. We hope to show the public at a later date, but now they’re busy.’

‘What a pity,’ said Mrs Bell, turning to Ju and Finbar. ‘But at least you two can swim in the aquatic centre, now we’re here.’

‘It’s closed,’ said Dr Lom quickly. ‘The robots are rehearsing there.’

‘In the swimming pool?’ said Mrs Bell.

‘It’s all right, Gran, we can go for a walk,’ said Ju, noticing that Dr Lom was looking disgruntled.

‘Since you’re here, Chloe,’ he said, ‘I’d like to discuss our problem with the latest animats. Perhaps they need additional instructions . . .’

Ju and Finbar slipped thankfully out of the building.

thirty-eight

LifeCorp's grounds were laid out with trees and bushes, and divided by tall hedges. The snow had settled and the ground was satisfyingly crunchy underfoot. Without realizing it, Ju and Finbar strayed off the gravel path and found themselves outside a flat-roofed building.

'Must be the aquatic centre,' said Ju. 'Look, Finbar! It's Eager!'

Two robots, one short and rubbery, the other tall and golden, were hurrying away from the building. They were carrying a stretcher between them.

'Someone's been hurt!' cried Finbar.

As he and Ju sprinted towards them, the stretcher-bearers began to swerve on and off the path, as if they couldn't decide which direction to take.

'Eager, what's happened?' breathed Ju. She saw that the stretcher was a sun-lounger. Underneath a pink towel appeared to be a body.

'We can't stop,' said the golden robot, who was at the front of the procession.

'I told you, they're my friends,' said Eager. 'Hello, Ju. Hello, Finbar. Are you here with Mrs Bell?'

'Yes,' said Finbar, taking his eyes off the sun-lounger.

'What is this? A tea party?' asked the golden robot.

'Of course not, Cedric,' said Eager. 'Shall I introduce you?'

'Why not make the sandwiches while you're at it!' stormed Cedric.

'Don't let us hold you up,' said Finbar, stepping to the side and pulling Ju after him. The robots hurried on.

'Has someone been hurt in the pool?' Ju called after them.

'No,' said Eager.

'Yes,' said Cedric, simultaneously.

Eager stopped walking and Cedric was obliged to halt too. 'Cedric,' said Eager, 'my friends might be able to help us.'

Finbar and Ju caught up with them. Finbar said politely, 'We'd like to help. What are you trying to do?'

'We're going to catch a hoverbus,' said Cedric, as if it was the most natural thing in the world.

'A hoverbus?' echoed Ju.

'Public transport is free,' said Eager. 'And the stop is just outside.'

'I know that,' said Ju. 'But you're carrying a stretcher – I mean, a sun-lounger – and what looks like a dead body.'

'Not dead!' exclaimed Eager. He looked upset.

Cedric put down his end of the sun-lounger. 'If you must know, we're carrying an animat. We plan to say she's broken down and we're taking her away.'

'That sounds plausible,' said Finbar. 'Even the sun-lounger makes sense, because you wouldn't need a proper stretcher for an animat.'

Cedric relaxed his guard. 'The problem is security at the main gate.'

Ju chewed her lip. 'But you're not a prisoner, Eager.'

'No,' said Eager, 'but . . .' He looked down at the covered figure on the sun-lounger.

'My status, and that of our animat friend, is less certain,' said Cedric. 'We intend to bluff our way out.'

'Ju and I could create a diversion,' said Finbar. 'Then you and the animat can run—'

'No,' said Eager and Cedric, in unison this time.

Finbar looked sheepish. 'You're right. It was a stupid idea. Security here is probably the tightest in the world.'

Cedric picked up his end of the sun-lounger. Eager followed suit and the robots quickly moved on. Ju and Finbar had to half-run to keep up with them. They rounded a hedge and the glass monolith reappeared. To the right of the headquarters was a row of hovercars.

Ju said, 'Can I ask why you are smuggling a—'

Finbar interrupted, pointing to the hovercars. 'They're taxis. Let's hire one and leave together. I'll pay.'

Cedric's finely sculpted jaw broke into a smile. Then he frowned. 'Will we get through the gate?'

'You stand more chance in a hovercar with us than on your own,' said Finbar.

'You're bound to be stopped otherwise,' said Ju.

'Perhaps,' said the BDC4. 'But people expect robots to be carrying things. The secret is to look purposeful.' He glanced ruefully at the bundle on the sun-lounger. 'Though it might be better to be carrying a refrigerator or something.'

'Cedric, we haven't much time,' said Eager. His voice was so full of anguish that Ju and Finbar looked at him in amazement.

'Come on,' said the BDC4, heading towards the hovercars.

They had to cross the front of the building. Through the glass could be seen Mrs Bell and Dr Lom walking towards the entrance, heads bowed as they chatted.

'They must be coming to find us,' said Ju. There would be no time for them all to get into a hovercar. 'I'll swap places,' she said. 'Get in.'

Cedric seemed to understand her plan. He opened the door of the nearest hovercar and scooped up the bundle from the sun-lounger. The towel slipped down, revealing an animat with pearly skin. Her slender arms clung to Cedric as he set her down on the back seat. He tucked the towel around her as

Finbar climbed in from the opposite side. 'Take us to the city,' the boy told the animat-driver.

'Aren't you going too?' cried Eager to Cedric.

'There's no time,' said Cedric. The hovercar, with Finbar and the animat, was gliding away.

Ju lay down on the stretcher.

'Ju! Are you all right?' Mrs Bell came running over, followed by Dr Lom.

'It's my ankle,' whimpered Ju. 'I tripped in the grounds, just outside the aquatic centre. Fortunately the robots saw me . . .'

'We were outside rehearsing,' said Cedric hastily. 'We fetched the sun-lounger.'

'Quick thinking,' said Dr Lom.

Mrs Bell had bent down to Ju. 'How bad is it?'

'I think I can walk on it now,' said Ju, with a sniff in her voice.

'What are you doing out here?' asked Dr Lom. 'When you were injured, why didn't you come straight back to headquarters?'

Ju's mouth fell open as she tried to think of an answer. She covered up by wincing.

'We'd better get you to first aid,' said her grandmother.

'I was just going to explain,' said Ju. 'Finbar forgot he has to meet his mum. He wanted to stay with me but I persuaded him to take the hovercar. Marcia gets very cross if he's late.' She looked up at Dr Lom. 'You've met his mother, haven't you?'

'Marcia Morris? Charming woman,' said the technocrat.

'Can we go home now?' said Ju, letting Mrs Bell help her to her feet. 'I think I'm able to walk. Can Eager come back with us?'

'If he wants to,' said Mrs Bell.

Dr Lom said, 'It's out of the question.'

Mrs Bell looked up in surprise.

'Miss Morris gave permission for Eager to come here, and I need her authorization before he can leave,' said Dr Lom.

Ju remembered the conversation outside the studio. She was tempted to remind the doctor that Marcia had said Eager decided for himself. She knew it would be pointless. She looked pleadingly at her grandmother.

'I understand, Dr Lom,' said Mrs Bell. 'Let's speak to Marcia later,' she told Ju.

'We'd better get back to the others,' said Cedric, leading Eager away.

'I'll come too,' said Dr Lom, glancing at his jinn. 'It's time for the performance.' He flashed a smile at Mrs Bell and Ju. 'Take care of that foot. I look forward to seeing you both when we present the show to the public.'

thirty-nine

Finbar was surprised how easy it was to leave LifeCorp's headquarters. The hovercar stopped at the gate as unseen security checks were carried out. Almost immediately the gate opened and the hovercar drove on. Finbar sat back in relief. The robot beside him couldn't be missing, after all. But what was he supposed to do with her? He couldn't take her to the Bells' house. Mrs Bell would be put in an awkward position, as she worked for LifeCorp.

His mother's studio was the obvious choice.

'The Hotel Regency,' he told the driver.

He turned to look at the animat. She sat upright, half-wrapped in the pink towel. Her face was human-like on a silver metal torso. She was extraordinarily beautiful. 'Hello, I'm Finbar,' he said. 'Who are you?'

The animat faced straight ahead, and said nothing.

Finbar wondered if she had heard. He repeated himself. She gave him a glance, cold enough to freeze his blood.

Gulping back shock, Finbar stared out of the window. This was a robot to be reckoned with! He pulled back the cuff of his coat. 'Jinn, get me Ju.'

Her face appeared on the tiny screen. 'Where are you?' she asked.

'On my way to see Mum,' he said.

'That's good,' said Ju. 'That's what I told Dr Lom and Gran. Listen, that BDC4, Cedric, and Eager are with us. We're all about to leave . . .'

'Come to the Hotel Regency then,' said Finbar. He couldn't wait to discover what was going on. It was clear that he wouldn't find out from the animat beside him. Though he fixed his gaze on the window, he couldn't resist another peep at her. She was so entrancing. The animat met his eye and gave him the same chilling stare.

Finbar kept his resolve never to glance at her again, until a sudden movement caught his eye. The pink towel had slipped down. Instead of slender ankles as Finbar expected, a tail, smooth and grey, was swishing against the floor of the hovercar.

Finbar was never more astonished in his life. He tried to speak, but his voice was caught in his throat.

'I'm a mermaid,' said the animat, in a musical voice.

Finbar managed to say, 'I can see that. Do you need to be in water?'

'Within the next ten minutes,' said the mermaid.

Finbar swallowed. He leant forward to tell the driver to go faster, and fell back against the seat. They'd better not be stopped for speeding. How would they explain a mermaid in the back to the police?

They were passing through the main shopping street. Large stores and billscreens competed for attention. Clothes floated, display dummies danced, and everywhere was a confusion of light, music and noise. People on the walking pavements bobbed up and down. Elsewhere, they stood chatting to billscreens as simulated creatures tried to sell them things.

The mermaid was looking out with incredulous eyes. Finbar said, 'It's too hectic for me. I prefer the stillness of mountains and lakes.'

She glanced at him, seemed to nod, and turned back to the window. Thankfully for Finbar, they entered the quiet road that led towards the Hotel Regency. His mother's studio was opposite. She kept a room at the hotel, which delivered food to her and did her laundry.

What now? thought Finbar. He could hardly go into the hotel with a mermaid, even supposing he could carry her. He called his mother on his jinn, praying she would answer. If she was in the middle of painting, she wouldn't.

'Hello, darling.' His mother's face appeared on the screen.

'Mum, I'm outside the hotel.'

She frowned. 'Is everything all right? Come over to the studio.'

'I can't,' said Finbar. 'There's someone with me and she can't leave the hovercar.'

'Is it Ju?' said Marcia.

'No. Mum, will you bring a bucket of water?'

Marcia raised her eyebrows. 'I'll be right down.'

Finbar turned to the animat. She seemed to be losing power. He would have been glad even of a frosty glare, but her exquisite green eyes had a faraway look.

'Hurry up, Mum,' said Finbar under his breath.

Marcia was at the hovercar's window, still wearing her paint-splattered overalls. Her hair was tied back with a silk scarf. She held up an old-fashioned kettle. 'Will this do?'

The mermaid's tail was flopping from side to side. Finbar pushed open the door, crying, 'It's a mermaid, Mum! She needs to be in water.'

Marcia looked into the car. For a picosecond, she hesitated. 'Overheating,' she said, and threw the contents of the kettle over the mermaid's tail. 'Driver!' she called. 'Come and get my luggage.'

Finbar looked at her with admiration. She was never thrown by technology, however unexpected. He supposed it was because she had been a technobrat, brought up with the latest gadgets.

Marcia was talking rapidly to the mermaid. 'I'm not going to harm you, I'm going to put you in the bath.'

'Bath?' said the mermaid weakly.

'A small pool.'

Marcia wrapped the towel around the mermaid and told the driver to hoist her over his shoulder. 'Now run into the hotel, driver. Gently.'

Finbar and his mother sprinted after the animat. They were halfway across the foyer when the manager appeared from his office. 'Good afternoon, Miss Morris. How is your work going?'

Breathlessly, Marcia said, 'I've just finished a sculpture. It's too big for the studio so I'm taking it to my room.'

'Can I help?' asked the manager.

'We'll manage, thank you.' She breezed past him without a second glance.

He called after her. 'Miss Morris, your sculpture is dripping.'

Finbar noticed they were leaving a damp trail.

'It's only water,' said Marcia, proceeding to the lift.

forty

Dr Lom and Hester walked down the tiled path beside the pool. Olga came forward with open arms.

'Welcome! Welcome to our performance,' she said.

'Where would you like us to sit?' asked the doctor.

'There is no need to sit,' said the robot. 'The performance is not very long. Please stand by the side here.'

Olga's greeting was so polished that Dr Lom nodded in approval. 'I almost wish we'd invited the public after all,' he told Hester. 'This could be very impressive.'

The robots were forming a group. Wag and Cedric, the tallest, went to the back; Olga stood between Eager and Wilf; the insects were in the front, on raised legs. Behind them rose the palm trees.

'It could be a holiday snap,' said Hester, fondly.

Dr Lom gave a laugh. 'Yes, they seem to be a close-knit team at last. Your choice of theme was an excellent one.'

The robots had arranged themselves. They stood still

for a moment, creating an air of suspense.

Hester whispered, 'Are they going to sing, do you think?'

Olga bowed her head. The audience could see her mouthing, 'One, two, three . . .'

In an explosion of sound, the robots chorused, 'FREEDOM!' as they gestured to the pool.

Dr Lom and Hester looked expectantly at the water, still believing that an entertainment would happen. A picosecond later, their faces fell. The robots kept their pose, arms pointing at the empty pool.

For a moment the audience was silent.

'I think I had better resign,' said Dr Lom quietly. 'The *Robot Einstein* think-tank is now closed.'

He turned and walked away, leaving Hester to remonstrate with the robots. 'What have you done with her?' she cried.

Olga stepped forwards. 'We have set her free,' she said patiently. 'It is a demonstration—'

'I did understand the point of your little exercise,' snapped Hester. 'Oh, what did we expect? You're only robots.'

'Yes, what *did* you expect?' asked Cedric quietly. He came close to Hester, and for a moment they looked at each other.

Hester said, 'You knew perfectly well what you were doing, didn't you?'

'Yes,' said Cedric.

She gasped and gave a little shake of her head. 'I think, as the project is now closed, you should all go home. I'll arrange for cars and pods to take you.'

The robots watched her leave in silence.

forty-one

Dulcie was in the bathroom of Marcia's suite at the hotel. She lay back in the bath as water flowed over her. Her eyes were closed. Marcia and Finbar stood watching her. Immersed in water, her silver metal torso and grey tail looked all of a piece.

'Strange hair,' said Finbar. 'I thought mermaids had long silky hair.'

'Mermaids don't exist,' said his mother wearily. 'She's a robot. Her hair looks like seaweed to me.'

'I wonder why,' he said.

'Finbar! Are you going to tell me what's going on?'

He sighed and sank down against the tiled bath. Marcia sat beside him. He told her about the visit to LifeCorp's headquarters and how he had met Eager and the BDC4.

'Next thing I knew, I was in the hovercar with the mermaid.'

'What happened to Ju?' asked his mother.

'She stayed behind with the robots. Dr Lom was running

towards us. But she was all right – Mrs Bell was there. I called her from the hovercar – they're on their way here.'

'Dr Lom saw you leave?'

Finbar nodded. 'But I don't think he saw the mermaid. She was crouched down.'

There was a loud splash and water poured over them. Marcia leapt to her feet with a shriek. A cool trickle went down Finbar's neck. He stood up, just in time to avoid a second cascade.

'Please stop splashing,' he said to the mermaid.

She was flopping her tail from side to side as if in distress, even though she was in water now. 'Where's the robot?'

'Which robot?' asked Marcia.

'The rubbery one.'

'Eager?' said Finbar.

The mermaid gave him the frosty look he knew so well. 'Yes – Eager. Where is he? I want to talk to him.'

Water still gushed from the taps. Dulcie began to strike her tail against the bath. Finbar could scarcely believe the din.

'Stop thumping,' said Marcia, 'and we'll fetch Eager. You'll empty the bath of water if you go on.'

The mermaid lay still, apart from the occasional swish of her tail. She eyed Marcia suspiciously. 'You'll bring Eager now?' she said in her melodic voice.

'He's on his way,' said Finbar.

The bath was full now and the taps turned themselves off. The mermaid closed her eyes again.

Marcia led Finbar into the bedroom, whispering, 'Have you no idea who she is, or where Eager and the BDC4 were taking her?'

Finbar shook his head. 'They just wanted to get her away, I think.'

'She doesn't seem very grateful,' said his mother, sitting down on the bed. 'I hope Eager gets here soon.'

Finbar sat on the sofa. 'What do you think she is, Mum?'

'A very expensive piece of equipment,' replied Marcia.

'A sea-bed explorer?' said Finbar.

His mother laughed. 'Far more sophisticated than that. She's the most up-to-date technology there is. She probably cost as much as a Sorbjet.'

'Oh,' said Finbar.

'And you appear to have stolen her.'

Finbar was taking this in, when a perky voice said, 'You have visitors . . .'

'Let them in!' said Marcia.

Mrs Bell and Ju entered, followed by Eager and Cedric.

'Marcia, what's all this about a mermaid? Can you explain what's going on?' asked Mrs Bell.

'I was hoping you could,' said Marcia. The BDC4 caught her attention.

Cedric stood in the corner, looking ill at ease. Eager remembered that even as a human he had been unused to company. He said, 'Cedric, these are my friends. You've met Finbar. This is his mother, Marcia Morris. She is going to marry Mrs Bell's son, Gavin.'

This was possibly more information than Cedric wished for. He gave Marcia an awkward nod.

Marcia said, 'I haven't seen a BDC4 for years.'

'He isn't like the others,' said Eager.

'Perhaps you and he could explain everything,' said Marcia.

'There isn't much to say,' said Cedric. 'The mermaid was put in the pool one night. She wouldn't tell us anything about herself, except that she'd been captured from the ocean. We decided to help her leave.'

'It's very odd,' said Ju. 'We met Dr Lom just now. We were with Cedric and Eager. He knew the mermaid had gone, but he didn't even mention it.'

'He looked ill,' added Mrs Bell. 'He said he was going to hand in his resignation! It's extraordinary. Half an hour before, we were chatting about work.'

'He's closed down *Robot Einstein*,' said Cedric. 'It's all because Dulcie has disappeared.'

'She hasn't disappeared,' said Marcia testily. 'She's in my bath.'

'But you won't send her back, will you?' cried Eager.

'She—' He was interrupted by the sound of thumping.

'It's the mermaid!' said Finbar. 'She wants to see you, Eager.'

Eager rushed into the bathroom. How could he have forgotten Dulcie? He had been too busy worrying about Cedric. He peered anxiously over the side of the bath.

Dulcie sat up and fixed her limpid gaze on him. 'So they fetched you, after all?' she said.

'They're my friends. You can trust them,' said Eager.

'Tell them to take me to the river, then,' said Dulcie. 'Let me go to the sea.'

'Of course,' said Eager. 'You don't belong here.'

The mermaid reached out and wrapped her fine metal fingers around Eager's wrist. Her grip was strong. 'Take me there and I'll tell you the truth.'

forty-two

Marcia was pacing the bedroom. 'Finbar, tell me again what happened when you left LifeCorp's headquarters.'

'Nothing,' said Finbar. 'We just drove out.'

'That was lucky,' said Ju.

'Strange,' said Marcia. She looked at Mrs Bell. 'If you had a robot worth millions, wouldn't you expect your security system to keep an eye on it?'

'Security is certainly tight at LifeCorp,' said Mrs Bell. 'There are scanners at all the gates.'

Marcia went on, 'So if Finbar wasn't stopped, it suggests the security system wasn't aware of how valuable the mermaid is.'

Finbar whistled. 'She's a secret, even to LifeCorp!'

Marcia tucked a lock of hair into her scarf. 'Dr Lom doesn't seem interested either. He must have realized by now that the mermaid left with Finbar. So why hasn't he called to demand her return?'

'Don't you have any ideas, Mum?' asked Finbar.

She sighed. 'My guess is, only a few high-level technocrats know who, or what, Dulcie is. That's why Dr Lom can't start a security alert to find her. He doesn't want to draw attention to her.'

Cedric nodded. He had ventured from the corner and was sitting on the bed beside Ju. 'Perhaps that's why she was brought to the swimming pool. Dr Lom could pretend she was part of the project, while waiting for orders.'

Eager came out of the bathroom. 'Dulcie wants to go to the river so she can swim to the sea,' he announced.

His friends looked at him.

Mrs Bell said gently, 'Eager, animats only say what they're programmed to say. Going to sea is Dulcie's job so she's bound to ask to go there. It doesn't mean she wants to go, in the way that *we* mean it.'

Finbar leapt in. 'We only call her an animat because she's got a human face. But she's intelligent in the way Eager is. You can tell she's got a mind of her own.' He looked from Mrs Bell to his mother. 'You're always saying that Eager must choose for himself – so should Dulcie.'

'Professor Ogden agrees with us about Eager choosing for himself,' said Marcia. 'But whoever built Dulcie may not want her to make her own decisions. They may want her back.'

'We can't ignore what she wants. That would be cruel!' cried Ju.

Marcia exchanged a glance with Mrs Bell. 'Robots and animals – the law is the same for both. Whether they're conscious or not, they belong to somebody and the owner makes the decisions.'

'But we don't know who her owners are,' Finbar reminded her.

'Then we'd better find out,' said his mother. '*Before* we throw their expensive hardware into the river. And even if Dulcie is self-aware,' she added, silencing Finbar's protest, 'we still shouldn't cast her into the sea. How will she survive? She could be dashed against rocks or swallowed by a whale . . .'

'She survived in the sea before,' said Eager. 'She has friends there.'

'If that's the case, I'd like to hear more,' said Marcia. 'But first, we need to find out who owns her. What do you think, Chloe?'

Mrs Bell nodded. 'Let's ask her now.'

'Is she really a mermaid?' whispered Ju to Finbar as they filed into the bathroom. Her mouth dropped as she saw the smooth silver tail.

The bathroom was very crowded with four people and three robots inside. Dulcie peered over the bath in astonishment. 'I don't know what you're waiting for,' she said. 'I don't jump through hoops.'

‘Please Dulcie,’ said Eager, ‘tell us who you are. We want to help you.’

She stared at the taps, as if weighing up the situation. ‘I’m a URA.’

Mrs Bell gave a gasp. ‘An Underwater Reconnaissance Agent?’

‘That’s right,’ said Dulcie, looking coolly at her. ‘LifeCorp built me to spy on the world’s governments. State buildings are often by water, it’s a pleasant spot to be. I can swim close and pick up their conversations.’

Eager’s system gave a start. Dulcie, a spy! He said, ‘Are there many of you?’

Her laughter bounced off the tiled walls. ‘Not after what happened! I was top secret. Only the highest technocrats knew about me. Even Dr Lom doesn’t know my real purpose. The technocrats bio-engineered dolphin cells to make my tail. They said there was no point trying to improve on nature. And they wanted to see whether they could do it.’

‘They succeeded handsomely,’ said Cedric. He stepped back, looking embarrassed.

Dulcie went on, ‘I learnt about the world from simulations—’

‘So did I!’ said Eager.

‘Then from my experiences,’ she said. ‘But I experienced the world like a sea mammal. I found I had feelings and thoughts and desires of my own.’

'Your dolphin half gave you consciousness!' exclaimed Finbar.

Dulcie smiled. 'But that wasn't the plan. LifeCorp immediately cancelled the programme to build more like me. They tried to destroy me, but the sea mammals helped me each time.'

'Destroy you!' said Eager.

'Then you were captured,' prompted Marcia. 'Why didn't LifeCorp destroy you then?'

Dulcie hesitated. 'I don't know.'

'Does LifeCorp own you, or did it build you for some government?' asked Mrs Bell.

'I don't know,' repeated the mermaid. She faced the taps again, a determined expression on her face.

The people in the room looked at each other. Finbar caught his mother's arm. He whispered, 'We can't send her back to LifeCorp to be destroyed.'

'She doesn't belong to us,' said Marcia.

'Mum!'

Mrs Bell sat on a stool. 'Aren't we overlooking something?' she said. 'If LifeCorp want to claim her, they've had plenty of time to contact us. But they haven't. In the next ten minutes, what's to stop Dulcie from going to the river and jumping in?'

Ju looked nonplussed. 'Her tail, Gran!'

'Precisely,' said Mrs Bell. 'It's the only thing stopping her. Now if we humans go home, and Cedric and Eager were to carry her to the river, who is to blame? They're only robots. And it wouldn't be our fault. We left a robot in the bathtub, in good faith.'

Marcia laughed.

'Brilliant, Gran!' said Ju.

There was a big splash as Dulcie slapped her tail against the water. Everyone jumped back. 'Stop talking and take me!' said the mermaid.

Finbar rubbed his eyes. So much discussion was making him tired, but he had a nagging thought. 'Hang on. What if LifeCorp expect her to go to sea? Perhaps they haven't bothered to come here because they're watching the river.'

No one spoke for a moment. Marcia said thoughtfully, 'People don't look for things that are staring them in the face.'

'Pardon?' said Ju.

'Sometimes, the best place to hide something is not to hide it at all,' said Marcia.

Finbar frowned. Now was not the time for his mother to become a Chinese sage.

She went on, 'The hotel manager thinks I've brought a sculpture to my room. So why don't I make one – a replica of Dulcie for the exhibition tomorrow? Let's show her to the world. I know! I'll invite Dr Lom to the opening so he can see her for himself. If he believes the replica is the real Dulcie, he'll call off any search for her. Meanwhile, the real Dulcie swims away. What do you think, Dulcie?'

All eyes were on the mermaid. 'A replica?' she said suspiciously.

'I'll need an hour, and I won't harm you,' said Marcia.

'Very well, but then I'm leaving,' said Dulcie. Her eyes fixed on Eager. 'You said I can trust your friends. I hope you're telling the truth.'

'I would never lie to you,' said Eager.

forty-three

Marcia went to her studio to prepare the materials she needed. Finbar offered to stay behind and help her. He said goodbye to Mrs Bell and Ju who went to catch the hoverbus home.

Cedric and Eager waited with Dulcie. She lay on her back in the bath, gently swishing her tail.

Curiously, Eager thought, she seemed smaller in the bath than in the swimming pool. There's more to her than her physical size, he decided. The water, her graceful movements, and the air above were as much a part of her as her tail. He began to understand why she longed for the vastness of the ocean.

She spoke. 'That man wanted your help, but he wasn't telling you the truth.'

'Dr Lom?' said Cedric.

'No robot can fix the weather,' said Dulcie. 'There's a problem with the water cycle because water itself is sick. Water reflects humans' feelings. There is too much discontent and greed in the world, so water needs to be healed.'

Eager remembered the words of the dowser.

The mermaid looked over the side of the bath. 'Technocrats have tried to restore the rainfall to the land. Whatever they do, fails. Already countries are squabbling over water and some are diverting their neighbour's rivers. Soon, there'll be wars.'

Eager and Cedric stared at her.

'The top technocrats are planning to leave – those who know that it's too late,' said Dulcie.

'Leave?' said Cedric. 'Go into hiding, you mean?'

'No, leave Earth.' Dulcie tossed back her hair.

There was a pause as the robots took this in.

'But where can they go?' asked Eager.

'To the moon,' said Dulcie, as if it was obvious. 'It already has living quarters and a robot factory. And there's no one there now. A year ago the technocrats sent everyone home, to leave the moon empty for themselves. They've been secretly sending up food and materials ever since.'

'No!' said Eager. 'People left because a signal came from outer space. Sam was there. ISA said he was a security risk because the signal might have come from aliens, and he was sent home.'

'The signal was a hoax,' said Dulcie. 'An excuse for ISA to change their personnel on the moon.' She slowly shook her head. 'I told you humans were duplicitous.'

There was another pause.

'How do you know all this?' asked Cedric.

'When I was spying I heard government ministers discuss it,' said Dulcie.

Cedric said, 'You mean, governments know all about it?'

'Only some very senior ministers,' said Dulcie. 'They're going to leave with the technocrats. Most ministers still think something can be done about the water cycle. That's why they ended the Ban – so intelligent robots could come out of hiding and help humans.'

'The President didn't say that,' said Eager.

'She wouldn't, would she?' said Dulcie. 'Governments want help from robots that think for themselves, but they won't admit such robots can exist!'

Eager nodded. Hester had said much the same thing at the *Robot Einstein* show. 'It's all very complicated,' he said.

'Of course it is,' retorted Dulcie. 'We're talking about humans.'

Cedric put his head in his hands. 'There's a problem with the water cycle; the land is drying up; the only people qualified to help are jumping ship . . . So there's nothing to be done.'

Dulcie sat bolt upright. 'What are you talking about? There's plenty to be done.'

The robots looked at her in astonishment. 'After all that you've told us?' said the BDC4. 'There's no hope.'

'There's no hope if we depend on humans,' said Dulcie. 'But something this important can't be left to them. They can't be trusted to agree among themselves, let alone do anything useful.'

'Dulcie, humans are always doing useful things,' said Eager. 'They built us, remember?'

'And who got Earth into the mess she's in?' asked Dulcie. 'Who cut down her forests and over-grazed the land? Humans always take more than they need, and then convince themselves that they needed the extra in the first place!'

Cedric said thoughtfully, 'You're a robot, built for the sea. Why do you care what happens on land?'

'It won't stop there,' said Dulcie, slapping down her tail. 'Humans have wasted Earth's water reserves and now they're turning to the sea – taking out the salt so they can drink it and irrigate their crops. As land finally turns to desert, they'll build floating homes on the ocean, with underwater chambers. The noise and pollution will be worse than ever. There'll be no place for the sea creatures. That's how humans are. They take over.'

Eager couldn't recall Mr and Mrs Bell taking over anything, in all the years he had known them. He said as much.

'What are two humans among billions?' asked Dulcie. 'They must all change—'

Cedric broke in. 'What are you proposing, Dulcie?'

She said slowly, as if the others spoke a different language, 'The whales, of course. They must sing their song.'

The robots stared at her. She said in exasperation, 'Everyone knows that whale song can heal water.'

'Can it?' asked Eager.

'Well, yes,' said Dulcie, sounding less certain than before.

'Years ago, if you'd told me that, I'd have laughed out loud,' said Cedric. 'But since working with my late owner, I can see there's truth in what you say. He believed that everything is vibration so sound, which is a particular kind of vibration, may well be able to retune water – if that's where the problem lies.' He began to pace the room. 'I can see a difficulty though . . .'

Marcia's voice called to them. 'I'm ready!' She came into the bathroom. 'You're the strongest, Cedric. Will you carry Dulcie down?'

She covered up the mermaid with the towel again and led the way to the lift. They made a striking procession across the foyer: Marcia, still in her paint-stained overalls, Eager looking anxious, and Cedric bearing his pink bundle. Several guests stopped and stared.

'Moving our sculpture again, Miss Morris?' said a voice behind them.

'It needs more work before tomorrow,' said Marcia. 'It's my most important exhibit.' She gave the manager a dazzling smile.

'By the way, I hope you can come to the opening. I'll put you on the VIP guest list.'

As Cedric waited for her, a large puddle was forming at his feet. The manager glanced down and opened his mouth to speak.

'It's only water,' said Marcia blithely. She led the robots out into the night.

forty-four

Marcia worked quickly, covering the mermaid with a white gel as she lay on a bench. Finbar and the robots watched from a corner of the studio, squeezed in among pots and canvases.

She took separate casts of Dulcie's torso, arms, and tail. Lastly, she did the head. 'Emerald,' she murmured, examining Dulcie's eyes. Within minutes, the gel had set. Expertly, she cut a fine seam along each cast, and prised it open.

'Do you need water yet?' she asked Dulcie. The mermaid shook her head. She swung her tail over the bench to give Marcia room to work.

Marcia joined the cut edges of the casts together and began to apply paint. Using her hands, she smeared a silver paste on to the torso.

Finbar loved to see his mother at work and was fascinated as the plain casts were transformed. But he couldn't stop yawning. It was late into the night.

'Go and sleep in the hotel,' said Marcia, without looking up.

'I think I might have to, Mum,' he said. 'But what's going to happen to Dulcie? She'd better not leave until after the exhibition opens tomorrow.'

Cedric piped up, 'I can carry her back to the hotel.'

'No,' said a voice.

They all turned to Dulcie.

'I'm not spending any more time in a bathtub,' she declared. 'I shall go to the river now.'

Finbar said, 'But LifeCorp might be patrolling the river. Wait until we've put the replica on display and let Dr Lom see it.'

'I'm running out of time,' said Dulcie. 'I shall risk it.'

'Then you'd better go,' said Marcia. 'I can't have you creating a rumpus in my bathroom again.' She gave a final scrutiny of the mermaid's face. 'All right, I can work without you now.'

Once again, Dulcie was covered in a towel and Cedric picked her up. Eager watched, his system still trying to make sense of what was happening. Dulcie was leaving that minute! It had been bad enough to think that she was going to swim away the following night. At least he would have had time to think what to say to her.

'Are you coming, Eager?' asked Cedric.

Finbar followed the robots out of the studio and pointed them in the direction of the river. It was a short walk away, behind the hotel. 'Bye, Dulcie,' he said. 'Good luck.'

The mermaid looked at Finbar, coolly. At least her gaze was a few degrees warmer than it had been in the hovercar, he thought.

'Thank you,' she said.

The robots came to a long embankment with steps to the river. Eager went first, glancing back at Cedric to make sure he kept his footing. The path was in darkness until they approached, when a row of slender lamps lit up along the bank. The glossy black river began to sparkle. Dulcie pulled the towel away from her face, as if she had sensed the water.

'Here?' said Cedric, looking up and down the river. There was no one about. The buildings on both banks were apartments and offices, their windows shuttered against the night.

Dulcie sprang from his arms, diving low into the river. For an instant Eager had an urge to jump after her. She reappeared, shaking her purple-black hair. The robots leant forward. 'In a minute,' she cried and plunged again.

Cedric whispered, 'How are we going to break it to her?'

Eager was intent on watching the surface for ripples. 'Break what?' he asked.

'The problem with her plan. I was telling you,' said Cedric. 'It can't work.'

Eager turned to the BDC4, horrorstruck.

'Her idea isn't novel,' said Cedric. 'People have made all sorts of claims about the power of whale song. Stories have been written about it. Thanks to my late owner, I'm inclined to believe the theory has something. But there's a simple reason why we'll never find out.'

'Go on!' cried Eager, forgetting to keep his voice low.

'Noise,' said Cedric. 'The whales' song needs to encircle the earth unbroken. But there's too much noise in the ocean these days for the whales to hear each other.'

'Noise?' said Eager.

'Human-made sound,' said Cedric. He ticked off on his metal fingers: 'Digging the sea-bed for minerals; ploughing up and down in their ships and yachts and fishing boats, day and night; dredging estuaries and using water for power . . . It never stops.'

'But humans care about other creatures,' said Eager. 'Why do they let this happen?'

'They try to improve their technology, to make less noise,' said Cedric, 'but they can't avoid it altogether. And don't forget the underwater laboratories, desalination plants, and deep-sea weapons testing. Their noise and vibration confuse the whales. Not only can't they hear their songs to each other, they also lose track of where they are.'

The water parted as Dulcie leapt up, headfirst, falling back with a splash. She smiled at the robots.

Cedric crouched down. 'Dulcie, why did you say you're running out of time?'

She hesitated. 'Some scientists suspect that the problem with the rainfall begins at sea, where clouds start to form . . .'

'It's a reasonable guess,' said Cedric.

'It may be,' said Dulcie, 'but when I was spying I learnt that governments are too desperate to wait and find out. They're going to try crazy measures to bring back the rain.'

'Such as?' asked Cedric.

'Releasing chemicals into the atmosphere, blowing up forests . . . They'll harm the planet, including the marine world,' said the mermaid. 'So if the whales don't sing soon, it may be too late.'

Cedric glanced at Eager. 'What if your plan doesn't work, Dulcie?'

'But it will,' she said, in surprise. 'The whales can heal the water. They always have done.'

Cedric said, 'I'm sure you're a magnificent Underwater Reconnaissance Agent, Dulcie. But you're one small mermaid in a huge ocean. How can you make this happen, even supposing it would work?'

'The whales are waiting!' cried Dulcie. 'They've been waiting for years. Their singing will heal, so long as the noise in the ocean is silenced.'

'Ah, yes, the noise,' said Cedric pointedly.

Dulcie bobbed in the water. 'If you would stop it, the whales could sing right around the earth.'

'*Us?*' exclaimed Cedric.

'That's what I wanted to ask you,' said Dulcie. 'You've both done so much – helping me escape and bringing me to the river. It would be a shame to come so far and not go a tiny bit further . . .'

'Tiny bit further?' echoed Cedric. 'How on earth do you expect us to stop the machines?'

Dulcie turned to Eager. There was enough light for him to see the green of her eyes. 'You can do it, can't you?' she said. 'What about asking Doug and Bug, the robots with so many legs? They're fault-finding robots. They could enter the gobetween and turn off the machines, or something.'

Eager wasn't sure about the insects, but he knew about Jonquil and the robots like him. He didn't think even they could do it, but not for the world would he tell that to Dulcie. 'Must we stop the machines for ever?' he asked.

Cedric shot him a look.

'Oh no,' said Dulcie. 'Not even a day. It doesn't take long for the singing to pass from whale to whale around the earth.' She flipped on to her side. 'I'll be off then.'

'Wait!' called Cedric. 'When do you think you'll reach the whales? What day should we stop the machines?'

She thought for a second. 'Two days, that should do it. That means Saturday – stop the machines on Saturday morning. Goodbye, Cedric. Goodbye, Eager.'

Her head went under the water. Before Eager could even think of what to say to the mermaid, she had disappeared.

forty-five

Dulcie kept close to the surface, now and again bobbing up to check her surroundings. However much a river snaked, it always followed a course to the sea. So surely she couldn't miss the sea if she swam straight on?

Although she had kept her promise to tell Eager the truth, there had been too little time to tell him *everything*. She hadn't told him, for example, that she didn't know how to navigate. As a reconnaissance agent, she had been taken out to sea or up a river then released to perform her mission. Afterwards, she swam back to the safety of the vessel.

When she escaped, she wouldn't have lasted long without the help of dolphins. They introduced her to marine life and led her to the ocean where she met other kinds of dolphins and whales.

Dulcie had expected these sea mammals to be lofty creatures compared to the humans she had known. She was disappointed to find they could be grumpy and argumentative. But they didn't spy on, or kill each other (apart from the aptly-named killer whales whom she learnt to avoid).

Over time, she grew used to the ways of the ocean. If a mammal had friends, they had a good chance of being protected against sharks and other predators, and Dulcie was treated as an honorary dolphin. They taught her how to dive and leap, and guided her in storm, wind and calm.

Now, for the first time, she was truly alone in the water. She had never experienced anything like this icy river with its fierce currents. It was too cold for sharks, which was a comfort. Despite the temperature, it was the summer season and whales would be in the sea this far north, but she had no idea where to look for them. She wasn't even sure that porpoises would be at the end of her journey to advise her.

Dulcie swam on, passing sour-faced fish who paid her no attention. The shifting currents slowed her down and forced her to change course many times. She would never reach the sea at this rate.

She bobbed up into the night. The sky was black and mottled with stars. A large boat went by, its deck lit up and music playing. She saw a crowd of people on board, eating and dancing, looking warm and happy. For a moment Dulcie was envious, not of their entertainment, but of their companionship. She knew she would always be an outsider, but she never felt this more keenly than when she saw humans playing together.

She dived and swam on.

forty-six

It was long past midnight. Eager was scarcely aware of his surroundings as he and Cedric walked back to the hotel. Everywhere seemed dark and empty, like the river after Dulcie had gone.

Cedric was talkative. 'Plucky little entity,' he said. 'I hope she soon finds her dolphin friends. They'll set her right about the whales.'

His last words drew Eager's attention. 'Set her right?'

'They'll explain to her that it's impossible to stop the noise in the ocean,' said Cedric.

'But we're going to stop it,' said Eager.

The BDC4 stared at him. 'Eager, I've told you! You don't really think Doug and Bug can help? Do you know how big the oceans are? How many machines?'

'I have a nephew . . .' began Eager. He quickly explained about Jonquil. 'He entered ISA's gobetween last year, which is top security, and altered a message. Perhaps he can connect to the machines at sea.'

Cedric shook his head. 'Even with humans' cooperation, nothing could be done in time. And we'd never persuade humans to believe in Dulcie's plan.'

'I wish I could ask Professor Ogden,' said Eager. He noticed Cedric's startled expression. 'Yes, he built me. And he helped design you.'

'Well, if he had anything to do with that nephew of yours, it might be worth a try. Where is this Jonquil?'

'Not far from where we first met,' said Eager.

They reached the hotel, just as Finbar crossed the road from the studio. 'Don't mention the whales,' whispered Cedric. 'Dulcie has swum away safely,' he told the boy.

'Move along,' said the animat-doorman, noticing the threesome huddled by the entrance. He recognized Finbar. 'I beg your pardon, sir.'

'Call a delivery pod for these robots,' said Finbar, with a yawn. 'I'm going into the hotel to sleep. I'll come to the Bells' house later. Will you be there, Cedric?'

'We're going on a trip,' said the BDC4.

Finbar was too tired to ask questions. 'See you at the exhibition, then. You'll be welcome to come.' He said goodnight and walked into the hotel, his legs on autopilot, just as a delivery pod arrived.

The robots flew over the sleeping city to the suburbs. They

sat in silence, their power turned down as they processed the day's thoughts. Cedric told the pod to land in the old professional quarter. 'Miss Morris' account,' he said, as they stepped out.

'Now where did I leave Orville?'

Eager looked at his companion in surprise. The road stretched ahead of them, empty of people and traffic, and well lit by streetlamps. It should have been obvious where the flying machine was parked. But Eager could see clearly that it wasn't there.

'Perhaps it's the next street,' he said helpfully.

Cedric paced the pavement, looking to the side. 'A wall. An old wall.' He quickened his step and Eager ran to keep up.

'It's in here!' hissed Cedric, stopping beside a brick wall. Young leaves sprouted over the top, suggesting a garden beyond. Eager peered along the length of the wall. There was no door.

Cedric pointed to the leaves. 'Bamboo. That's where I left it.'

'Did you fly into the garden?' asked Eager, wondering why the machine hadn't flattened the bamboo.

There was a scrape of metal as Cedric hauled himself over the wall. He reappeared with a stick of bamboo in his hand. 'I rolled up Orville and planted it,' he said, landing beside Eager. 'I didn't think anyone would be out chopping bamboo in this weather.'

It took Eager a moment to realize that he was looking at Orville. He reached out and touched the slender golden pole. 'Flexi-metal?' he guessed. He had only seen it used for lexiscreens before.

Cedric nodded. 'The controls are embedded in the fabric.'

'So this is why the patrol didn't take Orville?' said Eager.

'That's right,' said Cedric. 'As soon as they spotted me, I rolled it up, shinned up the wall and thrust it into the bamboo.'

'Wasn't the patrol surprised that Orville had vanished?' said Eager.

'They were animats. Unfortunately, I couldn't outwit them any further and they hauled me into their flying pod.' Cedric stepped off the pavement, checked there was no one about, and began to unfurl the flying machine. Stretched to its full length, it sprang back to shape. Out popped a golden muzzle, followed by a pair of stubby wings.

'Hop in,' said Cedric. 'I'll set the controls to retrace our flight the other day.'

They flew by little more than moonlight. The landscape below was an undulating shadow. Once again Eager thought of Dulcie. How swiftly and purposefully she had swum away – back to her own world.

forty-seven

Orville cast a beam on the countryside below. The snow must have melted, for the light was swallowed by darkness. Eager just recognized the fields by his home.

'We need to fly left,' he said. 'You'd better land on the hill. There's a wood at the bottom.'

Eager had not expected to be back so soon. Yet he felt he was a different Eager to the one who had left recently. He stood on the hill, looking down at the wood, feeling the wind blow.

Cedric rolled Orville into a pole and held it firmly as they went down the slope. Frost was still in the ground, which helped them to keep their footing. The sensors had recognized Eager and a gap opened in the hillside. The robots squeezed through. Cedric leant Orville against the wall of the tunnel.

'Eager!' Allegra's voice rang out. The robots hurried into the bright room where she stood waiting.

Eager introduced his sister to the BDC4. If she was

surprised to see Cedric, she didn't show it. 'Where's Jonquil?' asked Eager.

The hollow ball flew in and perched on his uncle's shoulder. 'What's happened? I saw you on *Robot Einstein,* Uncle Eager! You were the cleverest robot there.'

Cedric tuned his hearing to Jonquil's frequency and caught the tail-end of his words. 'I understand you're remarkably clever too,' he said. 'We need your help.'

Eager told Allegra and Jonquil how he had met Cedric, how he came to enter the show and go to LifeCorp's headquarters. He started to explain about Dulcie but for some reason his words became jumbled. Cedric took over. He recounted what the mermaid had said about the water, and how the whale song might help.

'Everyone on the gobetween is discussing the weather,' said Jonquil. '"Try this, try that", but still it won't rain properly. Couldn't you work out why not, Uncle Eager?'

'No,' said Eager.

Allegra turned to Cedric. 'You said you need Jonquil's help. What can he do?'

Cedric explained about the noise in the ocean from machines. Allegra said nothing. Eager was not surprised, as she was always reflective. But Jonquil's response, or lack of it, startled him. His nephew was draped over the professor's chair, where he hung listlessly.

Eager said, 'You can help, can't you, Jonquil?'

'I'd like to, but I don't think I can,' said his nephew. 'Our fault-finding robots can't influence machines all over the world. If there was a central gobetween that controlled them all, we could enter it. But there isn't one.'

Cedric went over to Eager. 'Don't be too downcast. We've done our best.'

Allegra said, 'Humans brought this trouble on themselves. They never know when to stop.'

Eager shook his head. 'If it is their fault, it's because they were trying to solve earlier problems. Humans mean well – most of them.'

He remembered one summer when he offered to cut the hedge in the Bells' garden. A clip here and there seemed to make no great impression; but suddenly he looked and there was little hedge left. Perhaps humans had done this with the planet. They had tried to mend their ways, but it was a slow tricky process. He didn't attempt to explain this to Allegra. Instead he said, 'We robots will suffer too, if the climate changes. We may not need air and water to survive, but we depend on the world as it is.'

'I wish I could help!' cried Jonquil.

Eager had an urge to be alone. 'Excuse me, Cedric,' he said.

Through the window in his room, he saw a night sky full of stars. Dulcie was swimming under the same sky, trusting in

Eager to silence the machines in the ocean. On Saturday, as she waited with her sea-creature friends, nothing would happen. A moment would come when she would know that Eager had let her down. He couldn't bear to imagine it.

forty-eight

The next time Dulcie surfaced, the sky was turning pink. On both sides of the river she saw ships, cranes and warehouses. Ahead of her the river broadened and disappeared into the sea. She turned on to her back, letting the current take her at last.

She bobbed up. Now where?

Any porpoises would probably be close to the shore. She was wondering which way to go when she noticed an island. Seals liked islands: they were handy for popping in and out of the water. And seals would know where to find porpoises.

Dulcie was so excited at the thought of meeting a friendly mammal that she dived from the water, forgetting it was dawn and she could be seen from the mainland. She raced across to the island. A young seal lay close to the water's edge. He must have just rolled over, for his upper half was wet.

She cried out, 'Friend!' in sea tongue, which was her way of introducing herself. The seal seemed amused, for he rolled over again and clapped his flippers, before poking his nose in her direction. He seemed ready to listen, though he said nothing.

'Where will I find porpoises?' she asked. 'Are they here?'

The seal spoke at last. 'To the north,' he said. Dulcie almost forgot to thank him in her haste to swim on.

'Oh, and if you see a whale, tell it to keep singing after midnight,' she called.

A cry followed her. 'Turn right!'

She swam up the coast, her eyes peeled for grey heads on the surface. Porpoises were unlikely to leap from the water. They were notoriously shy and rarely drew attention to themselves.

Half an hour later, she turned on to her back, frustrated at the failure of her search. The next moment the sea was full of clicking and squeaking – dolphins chatting to each other. She dived down, following the sounds.

There were two of them. Dulcie saw from their pale bellies and hooked fins that they were bottle-nosed dolphins. They were arguing amiably.

'I still think it's quicker to go to Normandy first, then the island, then the fishing grounds, and back,' said one.

'I disagree,' said the other. 'It's a shorter route to go to the island *before* Normandy and the fishing grounds.'

The mermaid circled them at a polite distance. 'Friend!' she said.

They swam right up, nudging her playfully with their beaks and squeaking excitedly.

'Are you a human?'

'She's some sort of dolphin, look at the tail!'

'So shiny,' said one, patting Dulcie's metal torso with her flipper.

Dulcie said, 'I'm a mermaid and I need to get a message to the nearest whales.'

The dolphin that had favoured Normandy said, 'I believe the nearest whales are south of the Emerald Isle.'

'Is that far?' asked Dulcie.

'Days,' said the second dolphin.

Dulcie said impatiently, 'That's no good. I need to tell them to start singing after midnight.'

The dolphins looked at each other. 'We saw a humpback off the south coast,' said one. 'He was spy hopping, so he might have been lost. We could go after him.'

'We still have to go to Normandy,' the other reminded her. 'It would definitely be better to go there first.'

'On the contrary,' said her companion, 'if we're going to the south coast too, it's quicker to go to the island, the south coast, the fishing grounds, and *then* Normandy.'

Both dolphins screwed up their eyes. Dulcie could tell they were concentrating very hard.

'I'm wrong,' said the first dolphin, opening her eyes. 'The shortest route between these four places is . . .'

'. . . the south coast first!' they cried together. 'Then the island, the fishing grounds, Normandy, and back again!'

They sprang from the water, spinning round and round. Dulcie wasn't sure whether they were pleased to have solved the problem, or just to have agreed finally. Perhaps it was both. She leapt after them. 'If you're going to the south coast . . .'

They fell back into the water, laughing and chattering. Dulcie dived after them. '. . . would you please start now?'

The dolphins were still engrossed in their play. There was no point in staying. She had better continue her search for porpoises. As she turned to leave, the dolphins came close, brushing her with their flippers; and she knew they had heard and understood.

She pushed away from them with a powerful move of her tail. Soon she surfaced to check that she was heading towards the shore. When she looked back, the dolphins were speeding away, clearing the sea in long low leaps.

forty-nine

Early in the morning Eager set off for the wood. Now the snow had melted, he wanted to see whether the stream had returned. He felt anxious: what if the water still wasn't flowing?

He hurried through the trees, restored to their summer green, to where the land sloped. Birds were still chirruping noisily after their dawn chorus. He concentrated on the one sound he wanted to hear, and there it was! A gentle, burbling whoosh. He ran. Behind the trees, skipping over the mossy stones, was the stream. It was like meeting an old friend again.

'Hello, stream!' cried Eager.

The crystal clear water bubbled out. Eager stood and watched. He began to feel joyful again, as if all was well with the world – the way he felt when Sphere appeared. Dulcie's plan might yet work, he thought. Perhaps the whale song could encircle the earth, despite the noise.

Presently it was time to go back. Cedric was waiting to take him to the Bells' house. As he passed the pine trees a miniature sun slipped out, dazzling him. Sphere! Its light subsided as Eager came closer. He was puzzled. Sphere appeared most often when he felt despair. But the stream had already lifted his mood. Had Sphere come for some other purpose?

The ball hovered, midair, until Eager drew level. Eager stopped, and neither of them moved. Eager walked on and Sphere floated beside him. It kept to his side all the way back to the compound. Eager paused for Sphere to go ahead, but the ball hung back as if saying, 'You first.'

Inside, Jonquil and Allegra were demonstrating the fault-finding robots to Cedric. They looked round, greeting the luminous ball in silence.

'It's Sphere,' said Eager.

Jonquil, who had been star-shaped, instantly became a ball to show his kinship to Sphere. The same machine had been used to partly build both of them. Sphere floated closer to Jonquil, as if to acknowledge the connection. It moved to the gobetween and hovered there.

A thought came to Eager, clearer than the spoken word would have been. 'Sphere has come to help us,' he said. 'It can stop the machines in the ocean.'

'That's possible,' Allegra said. 'A quantum phenomenon like Sphere could influence the gobetweens all over the world, simultaneously.'

Eager looked at Cedric. 'I very much hope that is so,' said the BDC4.

In all his existence, Eager had never been let down by Sphere. If Sphere had come to help, Dulcie's plan must be the right one. But a thought struck him. 'Sphere, it's important that humans aren't hurt when the machines stop. There may be hospital ships or people needing help at sea. What will happen to them?'

Cedric said, 'The machines will only be without power for a few hours.'

Eager knew that very sick people or newborn babies often depended on machines. A few hours could be too long. Sphere began to glow, its rays spreading like flames. They died down.

'I understand, Sphere,' said Eager. 'You'll keep the power going where it's needed.'

'Shall we go?' asked Cedric.

Eager thanked Sphere and said goodbye to his robot family. Allegra stood at the door to the tunnel, with Jonquil on her shoulder. 'When are the senior technocrats leaving?' she asked.

Eager was slow to understand.

Cedric said, 'You mean, to go to the moon? Dulcie didn't say.'

Eager said reassuringly, 'Professor Ogden won't be one of them, Allegra.'

'I didn't think that,' said his sister. For the first time ever, she took his hand. 'Goodbye, Eager.'

Jonquil's shrill voice called after him, 'Goodbye, Uncle Eager!'

fifty

Finbar spent the night in his mother's hotel suite. The next morning, when he peered into the main bedroom, he saw that Marcia hadn't slept there. He pulled on his clothes and hurried downstairs. The hotel bustled with activity as guests came and went for breakfast or set off for the day.

He crossed the road. The studio was in darkness: Marcia must have closed the blinds. There was no sign of her. He was reluctant to pad around the room in case he crashed into something.

A light came on and he gave a cry. Dulcie was still there! She lay on the bench, looking up at him with an expression both frosty and playful. His befuddled brain corrected itself. It must be the model of the mermaid. He admired her glistening tail and the blue tinge of her skin. 'It's brilliant,' he said.

'Good,' said a voice, yawning.

Finbar swung round. His mother was curled catlike on the sofa. 'You must have worked all night, Mum.'

'Yes.' She yawned again.

He went closer to the replica mermaid. At that range, he could see all the evidence of the artist's hand.

And unlike the real Dulcie, the imposter never moved. He chose his words carefully. 'How are you going to display her? Because, of course, she's more convincing from a distance.'

'There's more to do. Don't worry,' said Marcia airily.

The filigree bracelet on her wrist began to trill. It was her jinn. 'Gavin is calling,' said a voice.

'Hello, darling,' said Marcia.

Finbar made to leave, but she shook her head at him.

'I hope you've had a good night's sleep,' said Gavin's voice.

Marcia began to giggle. She covered her mouth with her hand but her laughter grew. Finbar couldn't stifle his laughter, either. His shoulders rocked.

Gavin was calling, 'Marcia! Marcia! Are you all right?'

'I'm fine,' said Marcia. 'I've a lot to tell you. Yes, I will be OK for the wedding. I do love you. I'll see you tonight.'

She wiped the tears from her eyes.

'You'd better get some sleep, Mum,' said Finbar.

Dulcie followed the coast, still looking for porpoises who might direct her to whales. She couldn't count on the bottle-nosed dolphins finding the humpback. She kept her eyes and ears open for other dolphins too. They might be more help than porpoises, as they were prepared to go far out to sea.

At midday Dulcie stopped and looked about her. A cold fine drizzle was falling. She despaired of finding any more sea mammals. Her hopes had been high when she set off down the river. Now success depended on a pair of argumentative dolphins, who couldn't go anywhere without first doing complicated arithmetic.

The mermaid bobbed on the water, lonely and lost. She thought she would even be glad to see the young seal again.

A boat was approaching. She felt the vibrations before she heard its engine, and dived quickly. The vibrations grew more powerful. The people on board were using sonar to find something. She could see the bottom of the boat. It was a small speed vessel, not the kind for fishing. What could they be searching for out at sea?

She went deeper, dodging the sound waves. The boat ploughed on, but she couldn't let it go without knowing its purpose. She swam after it, tuning her ears to the frequency of the human voice.

Eventually she picked up the conversation on board. A deep voice was saying, 'We know she's here. How fast can a robot swim?'

A higher voice said, 'It's like looking for a needle in a haystack. We need a tracker boat.'

'Or a whaleboat!' The man gave a grim laugh.

Dulcie was galvanized. She swam to the sea-bed, fighting her way through seaweed. The people were looking for her! How did they know she was there? She couldn't think how anyone might have seen her from the shore.

Her thoughts raced. Dr Lom hadn't seen the replica mermaid yet, and meanwhile he'd sent a search party to the river. Or perhaps the woman had only pretended to make the replica, to trap Dulcie. Humans could never be trusted. Yet the robot with the kind eyes had assured her that his friends would help. Had they deceived him too?

But the man on the boat had said: 'We *know* she's here.' There was only one way he could know for certain – Eager and Cedric had betrayed her to LifeCorp! Dulcie remembered how earnestly the robots had offered to help. Two-timing machines! They were no better than humans. She might be half-robot herself, but she would never trust a robot again.

There was still the danger the boat would come in her direction. Dulcie turned tail. On and on she swam, ignoring the curious fish that clustered about her. At last she was satisfied that the boat was far ahead. Yet from the conversation she had heard, the humans would carry on looking for her.

Dulcie flipped on to her back, letting herself drift in the water. The whole sky was grey. She longed to go home, but where *was* home? More importantly, where was she? The shoreline had disappeared, and there was nothing around her but sea.

fifty-one

Flying over the countryside once more, Eager repeated the good news to himself. Sphere and Jonquil would silence the machines in the ocean, and Dulcie's whale friends would finally sing around the earth.

Though Eager would never see the mermaid again, she would know that he had not let her down.

Cedric leant back in the pilot's seat. 'That floating ball must be a quantum supersolid,' he said. 'My late owner would have loved to see it. As for Jonquil and the fault-finding robots, they could make Professor Ogden's fortune.'

Eager broke off his thoughts. 'Professor Ogden said the world isn't ready for the robots. They make him think of Prometheus.'

Cedric laughed. 'Professor Ogden's like Zeus, afraid that humans will misuse the technology. Fire was put to many good uses, but humans also produced firearms and nuclear bombs.'

'What harm can fault-finding robots do?' asked Eager.

'If they can correct a fault, they can also introduce one,' said Cedric. 'In the wrong hands, they could create chaos in the world.'

He noticed Eager's crestfallen expression. 'Don't worry! There are always two sides to everything. Life is about trying to find a balance between them. Look at me! I'm still torn between my human memories and my robot body.'

Dulcie has two sides, thought Eager. Sometimes she's cross and sometimes she looks pleased with me . . .

'I'll drop you in the old professional quarter, shall I?' Cedric was saying.

'Aren't you coming to the exhibition?' said Eager. 'We can leave together from the Bells' house.'

'No, I must go on,' said Cedric.

'Home?' asked Eager.

A transformation came over the BDC4. He shifted in his seat and looked around him, as if unsure where to fix his gaze. 'I'm . . . um . . . going to Olga's house.'

'To see Olga?' said Eager.

'Well, er . . . to live there. Her people are scientists, like my late owner. She thinks I could be their assistant,' said Cedric.

Eager remembered the man and wife on the *Robot Einstein* show. 'I've seen the people. They seem very friendly.'

Cedric said hesitantly, 'Olga is no scientist . . .'

'No,' agreed Eager.

'She has other talents,' said Cedric.

'Yes,' said Eager.

'Very sympathetic,' said Cedric.

'Yes,' said Eager.

'Kind,' added Cedric. They had reached the city suburbs and he set the controls to land. He glanced at Eager. 'We're friends, aren't we?'

'Yes,' said Eager firmly. He realized he no longer had misgivings about the BDC4.

'Let me give you some advice then,' said Cedric. 'Don't let anyone know about Dulcie's plan. Human, robot, friend or foe – don't mention it.'

'What about the Bells, Professor Ogden . . . ?' asked Eager.

'Well, you must decide,' said Cedric. 'It makes no real difference who you tell, because no one will believe you.'

Eager was silent.

'My late owner was an exception,' said Cedric. 'I don't know how many like him there are. But most people will think you're away with the fairies, as my mother used to say.'

Eager wondered idly whether fairies were as large as angels. 'Thank you for the advice, Cedric.'

It was late afternoon and the streets below were busy. Orville touched down in a quiet cul-de-sac.

'I'll keep in contact,' said Cedric, as Eager climbed out.

'Give my best wishes to Olga,' said Eager. He waved goodbye until Orville was airborne again.

fifty-two

The lawn outside the Bells' house was dotted with yellow. Eager took a moment to realize that the lime tree had shed its blossom. The front door opened. 'So you're back,' hissed a voice. 'Hurry inside, I need your help.'

'What for, house?' asked Eager.

The door closed behind him. 'I've written a poem to celebrate the marriage of Gavin and Marcia . . .'

The wedding! Eager had completely forgotten that it was the next day.

'I'm not too sure about it,' said the house. 'Let me tell you, before everyone comes:

> 'Had I no eyes but ears, my ears would love
> That inward beauty and invisible—'

Eager interrupted. 'Are you sure you wrote this, house?'

'Of course,' said the house. It went on:

> 'Or were I deaf, thy outward parts would move—'

Finbar's voice called, 'Eager's back!' The boy bounded downstairs. He was dressed in the clothes he had worn for the *Robot Einstein* show. The house fell silent.

Mrs Bell came out of the kitchen. 'Did you enjoy yourself?' she asked. 'Finbar said you were going on a trip.'

'We went to see Allegra and Jonquil,' said Eager.

Finbar said, 'Mum's finished the replica of Dulcie. It's just like her. Let's hope the real mermaid is well out to sea by now.' His mouth fell when he saw the robot's doleful expression.

'It's where she belongs,' said Mrs Bell. 'The sea is her element.'

The robot gave her a pained look. Mrs Bell and Finbar exchanged a look. They began to chat to him both at once.

'Ju's gone home,' said Mrs Bell.

'Ju's mum and dad came back this morning,' said Finbar.

'Fleur is furious with Marcia and Gavin,' added Mrs Bell. 'She thinks they should have told her they were seeing each other.'

'I expect it's better to fall in love without your friends and family watching,' said Eager.

Mrs Bell looked surprised. 'That's exactly what I told her.'

A horn beeped outside. 'There's Peter,' said Mrs Bell. 'He's hired a hovercar to take us to the exhibition. Are you two ready?' She led the way down the garden path.

'Welcome home, Eager!' called Mr Bell.

The robot climbed into the back of the hovercar beside Finbar.

'You had an eventful time at LifeCorp, I hear,' said Mr Bell. 'What's all this about a mer—?'

Mrs Bell silenced him with a shake of her head. He gave a puzzled frown and concentrated on driving.

fifty-three

The art gallery had once been a market hall. Eager paused to look at the lacy ironwork above the entrance. Inside, steel girders supported the lofty roof.

Rows of pictures, artfully lit, made him think of sunshine, or the sky at night, or a wood in autumn; even though Marcia had not painted these things directly but as bold strokes of colour. Eager marvelled at the power of humans to create beauty. Even the cityscape was beautiful in its way. Humans seemed driven to make things and transform their surroundings. But as Allegra had said, they didn't know when to stop.

Mr and Mrs Bell were busy discussing the pictures.

'I'm going to find Mum,' said Finbar. 'See you later, Eager.' He kept his head down as he threaded his way through the guests.

Marcia was with Gavin, laughing at something Rick Rhodes had said. Finbar thought she looked radiant. No one would ever guess she had been up all night. She caught sight of her son and came over to him. 'Finbar darling, let me show you the finished result.' The crowds fell back as she swept him to the centre of the gallery. In a large tank of pink water floated the replica Dulcie.

'It's perfect, Mum,' said Finbar quietly. 'Though I suspect pink isn't Dulcie's colour.'

But it did the trick. The water and glass disguised the artist's handiwork. They even created an illusion of movement. The effect was so strong that the mermaid seemed to swish her tail. It happened again, and Finbar frowned. 'Mum, did I just see . . . ?'

Marcia led him aside, whispering, 'Animatronics. Basic stuff. We want Dr Lom to believe it's the real thing, and Dulcie would never be still for two weeks.'

'Did you do it?' asked Finbar.

'No. Last week I called Fleur to invite her and Sam to the wedding. I remembered they were coming back early today, so I asked Sam to help.' Marcia smiled. 'Everyone should have a technocrat in the family.'

'You haven't married Gavin yet,' said Finbar. He could tell she was impatient to get back to him. As she turned to go, a posse of reporters arrived. 'Miss Morris, do let me have a picture with the mermaid behind you!' said one.

'The mermaid is a statement for our time, do you agree, Marcia?' asked a woman reporter. 'Where is the boundary between what's natural, and what isn't? *Is* there a boundary?'

Finbar's mother positioned herself by the tank. The photographer clasped a lens to his eyes and blinked to start capturing the image. Marcia smiled and tossed back her hair until he stopped recording. 'I'm sure we'll find a striking shot among that lot,' he said.

A guest had wandered over to the tank and was staring at it. The glass of wine in his hand seemed forgotten.

'Dr Lom!' said Marcia. 'Mind you don't spill wine on your suit! I'm delighted you could come.'

He gave her a clipped smile.

'But please excuse me, people are waiting for me . . .' Marcia slipped away.

Finbar admired his mother's cool. But even she wasn't brazen enough to chat to Dr Lom beside the replica mermaid. He wished he'd hurried away too. How could he look Dr Lom in the eye, knowing that the man knew he had fled with Dulcie?

Luckily, the newswoman stepped between them. 'Dr Lom, we'd love to hear your views!' She spoke into her jinn: 'Dr Lom, Head of Robotics at LifeCorp . . .'

'I've resigned,' said the doctor.

'Correction, Jinn . . . Dr Lom, *former* Head of Robotics at LifeCorp . . .' The newswoman looked up at Dr Lom again. 'This sculpture is science fiction, of course. But scientists have already combined animal cells with machines. Is it the future of robotics?'

Dr Lom said through clenched teeth, 'It may well be.'

Finbar went to find Ju.

Ju arrived with her parents. Since Sam had helped to install the replica he was able to lead them straight to the tank. Unsure what to expect, Ju grinned when she saw the mermaid's haughty yet playful expression. 'That's just how Dulcie looks,' she whispered to Sam and Fleur.

Sam put his arm around Ju. 'Sorry I've been so busy today. I'll cook supper later and you can tell me what's been happening.'

'It's all about Eager,' said Ju.

'Where is he?' asked her mother.

A boy in a red taffeta shirt, accompanied by a large robot, came up to the tank. Ju recognized Wag before she realized the boy was Dean Elliot. What a cheek! All last summer he'd visited art galleries pretending to be Marcia's son. How dare he even come to her exhibition, let alone on the opening night when Finbar would be here! At least he can't be impersonating him tonight, she thought wryly. But I'd better warn Finbar he's here.

'Can we have a picture of the robot?' a man with a press badge was saying. 'He won *Robot Einstein,* didn't he? Let's put him next to the mermaid. What a lovely couple!'

Ju touched her dad's arm. 'I'm going to find Finbar,' she said. The gallery was filling up and she had to dodge people as she hurried on past the paintings. Two large men blocked her way.

'My favourite picture is near the entrance,' one of them was saying. 'I went for another look, and a robot is right in front of it. I told him to move but he just stands there!'

'I wonder if he's part of the exhibition,' said the second man. 'There's another robot in that tank over there. Some kind of fish . . .'

Ju went the other way, avoiding glasses of wine, waving arms, and animats with serving trays. At last she spotted Eager before a painting. She glimpsed soft blues and greys, shimmering with gold, which recalled the sea at sunset. 'Eager,' she said gently.

He turned round, the most sorrowful expression on his face. Ju caught sight of Finbar and gave him a helpless shrug behind Eager's back.

Grinning, Finbar came up to them. 'Dr Lom's in a state of shock. He thinks he just saw the real Dulcie.'

'You mean, the replica has worked?' exclaimed Eager.

'Looks like it,' said Finbar. 'So LifeCorp can't have recaptured the real mermaid – unless Dr Lom is double-bluffing us. Which isn't likely,' he added hastily, noticing Eager's distress.

Ju said, 'I'm sure Dulcie is safe. She's probably out at sea with friends by now.'

Eager stepped back from the painting. 'Where is the replica mermaid?' he asked.

A glance passed between Ju and Finbar. 'Come and walk round with us first,' said Finbar, leading him in the opposite direction to the tank. 'We might meet someone we know.'

fifty-four

The gallery was chock full of people. Those who weren't admiring the paintings stood in tight groups, chatting noisily. Ju noticed her parents in the far corner and steered Eager towards them.

'Eager, welcome back!' cried Fleur.

'About time too,' said Sam.

Eager asked, 'Did you enjoy your holiday?'

Fleur began to describe Scotland. Relieved that Eager was distracted, Ju looked round for Finbar. He had his back to her, facing the mermaid's tank, where Dean Elliot stood. Ju whispered, 'I was about to tell you he was here. How dare he?'

Finbar shrugged. 'I half expected it. He's fascinated by Mum. I think he genuinely likes her paintings.'

Ju was amazed at his calm. 'Have you forgiven him again?'

'He hasn't done anything, except win *Robot Einstein*,' said Finbar. 'But I'd like to know where he got that robot.'

Finbar sidled through the crowd to get to Dean Elliot. He

stopped dead when he saw that Dr Lom was still by the tank, talking with Rick Rhodes.

'Hi Finbar,' said Dean, as if they were old friends.

Standing behind Finbar, Ju swallowed her indignation. She hoped he wouldn't introduce her. She would never keep her temper.

'Congratulations on winning the show,' said Finbar. 'Who built your robot?'

'My dad and his colleagues,' said Dean.

Finbar was surprised. He knew that Dean's father was a hacker, stealing information on the gobetween. Hackers exploited other people's machines, rather than building their own.

'Dad likes designing things,' said Dean. 'Of course he kept Wag secret during the Ban.'

Finbar nodded.

'It's a pity the think-tank closed,' Dean went on. 'We were hoping Wag would become world famous. Still, just winning the show has made him a household name. Dad's fixing a tour for him – the world's first robot stand-up comedian!'

'You're joking,' said Finbar.

'No, I'm not,' said Dean. 'We're going to program him with regional jokes, to tell in different parts of the country.'

'Program him?' exclaimed Ju, stepping forward in spite of herself. 'So he is nothing but a joke machine?'

Dean looked offended. 'Programming him is like giving someone a script to learn. Human stand-up comedians memorize their routine. They don't make it up as they go along.'

'At least comedians understand what they're saying,' said Finbar.

'Didn't you hear the judges?' countered Dean. 'If you find something funny, it shows you understand how the world works.'

'But does Wag know that he's making a joke?' asked Ju. 'If he doesn't, then he doesn't understand about the world.'

Dean scowled. 'Well, who cares? He's going to make us a mint.'

Wag lumbered over to them. 'I've just said hello to Dulcie,' he said.

'Who?' asked Dean.

'The mermaid,' said Wag. 'But there's something wrong with her.'

Finbar caught his breath. He felt Ju's hand on his arm, the fingers digging into his flesh. He remembered that Dr Lom was in earshot.

'What do you mean?' asked Dean, frowning.

Dr Lom seemed to have broken off his conversation.

'She's not right,' said Wag. 'You need to open her up.'

Ju's grip on Finbar's arm tightened.

'There's only one thing to do with that fish,' Wag went on. 'Take her to a stur-geon!'

Dean burst out laughing and gave Finbar a look that said, 'I told you so!'

Finbar glanced at Dr Lom and saw he had resumed his conversation with Rick Rhodes. He began to laugh too. Ju joined in, as if Wag's joke was the funniest she had heard in ages.

'I'm glad you're enjoying yourselves,' said Marcia, coming up to them. 'I'm going home to get some beauty sleep.' She smiled at Dean.

'This is Dean Elliot,' said Finbar. 'He owns Wag.'

As Marcia went to shake his hand Dean blurted out, 'I adore your paintings, Miss Morris. They're so vibrant. When I look at them, it's like hearing someone singing their heart out.'

'Thank you,' said Marcia, looking pleased. 'From the way you dress, you enjoy colour too. Do you paint?'

He shook his head. 'I'm just a connoisseur.'

She laughed. '*Just* a connoisseur? You're very important. It's lovers of art who buy my paintings.'

'I'll buy one, one day,' said Dean gravely.

He will too, thought Finbar, once Wag has earned a fortune.

When Marcia had gone, the boy turned to him. 'Well, see you around maybe? Why don't I send you some tickets for one of Wag's shows?' For an instant he looked boyish and uncertain.

Finbar smiled. 'Yeah, why don't you?' he said.

fifty-five

Dulcie was well and truly lost. It was late in the day and the sun was sinking. She knew it was possible to navigate by the stars when they appeared, but she had never learnt how. In any case, grey clouds were covering the sky.

The water grew choppy. She hoped a storm wasn't coming. Her greatest fear was to be dashed against rocks, her metal torso and its circuitry crushed. Where could she shelter? She remembered the places the dolphins had mentioned. But what was Normandy and where was the island they spoke of?

The sea turned dark. A huge shadow was coming towards her. Was this the storm? 'Too cold for sharks,' she kept repeating, although that was no guarantee. Fish scattered in their thousands, hitting Dulcie like heavy rain. She dived beneath them, as a great bulk swept over her.

Everything went black. She heard the deep groan of an adult whale.

He'd better not be hungry! thought Dulcie. If he opened

wide his massive jaws to swallow plankton, she and everything else would end up inside. But a whale was just what she needed. As it would be foolhardy to greet him head-on, she swam along his length, and was delighted to see the long white flippers of a humpback.

Gripping hold of the fin on his back, she pulled herself on to the hump as he rose out of the water. She dragged herself along his stout body, her tail slithering behind her. At last she reached the top of his head.

The next moment, she was tossed into the sky by two jets of air. 'Hey!' she cried, tumbling backwards.

She should have known better: the whale had broken the surface to breathe out. She bobbed in the water, admiring the wide plume of his blow. When the vapour died away, she swam to him quickly, before he plunged again. She looked for the opening above his eye and shouted in his ear, 'Friend!'

The whale raised his head a fraction.

'Friend!' bellowed Dulcie.

'I beg your pardon, I didn't quite hear,' said the humpback.

'Friend!' Dulcie cried again. With a push of her tail, she swam into his line of vision.

'I'm delighted to meet you, Friend,' said the whale. 'I wonder if you could help me. I appear to have lost my way.'

'I'm lost too,' said Dulcie. 'Haven't you met the dolphins?'

'I didn't have that pleasure,' he said.

Dulcie slapped her tail in frustration. 'Perhaps they went to Normandy first, after all.'

'I don't know about Normandy,' said the humpback. 'I'm on my way to the Emerald Isle. At least, I *was*.'

'It's a long way, I know that,' said Dulcie.

'My friends are waiting for me there,' said the whale. 'Fellow humpbacks, and some rather charming fin whales.'

This was music to Dulcie's ears. 'Why don't you sing a message to your friends, asking them to guide you?'

'Hadn't thought of that,' said the humpback. 'I usually sing when it's time to find a mate – love, that sort of thing.'

'I see,' said Dulcie. She made a quick calculation. Whatever happened, the whale would never arrive before tomorrow. 'Could you sing them another message, as well?' she asked. 'Tomorrow the humans will stop making noise in the ocean. Then you whales can sing and your songs will circle the earth again.'

The humpback moved his long snout up and down. Afraid, once more, that he would open his mouth wide, Dulcie swam to a safe distance. 'The good old days,' he said, becoming still again. 'My mother told me about them.'

For the first time on her mission, Dulcie's conviction wavered. She swam back. 'Is it true, then? You can heal the oceans?'

'Allow me to explain,' said the humpback. 'Everything

is vibration, even matter, when it comes down to it. Our whale song happens to vibrate at the perfect frequency for water. It's probably no coincidence, of course, as water is our element. If water is out of balance, our singing will restore it to health.'

'And the water cycle will go back to normal?' asked Dulcie.

'I'm not sure about that,' said the humpback.

Dulcie nodded. 'That's what other whales have told me.'

'However, I remember my mother saying something about it. What was it?' His snout began to nod again. The long folds of skin underneath were flapping in the water. Dulcie was about to dive away when the movement stopped.

'Oh yes. Space. She said that water is the antenna for energy from space. Does that help?'

'I don't know,' said Dulcie, who was now feeling confused. 'But could you tell your friends to begin singing tomorrow?'

The whale said, 'I could tell them anything if only I was just across the sea from them. A few hours ago I thought I was on course, but I came across these tall machines . . .'

'Water turbines?' suggested Dulcie.

'Possibly,' said the humpback. 'Didn't know whether I was getting a signal from a friend, or vibrations from those contraptions. I must have taken a wrong turning then.'

'Well, where do you need to be?' asked Dulcie, impatiently. The darkening sky told her there was little time left.

'The Toe,' said the humpback. 'I swim around the Toe and if I go out far enough I'll pick up a warm current to take me north.'

'And then you will sing your song?' said Dulcie.

'Yes,' said the humpback.

The mermaid thought for a moment. 'The machines in the ocean will only be quiet for a morning. Will that give the whales enough time to sing around the earth?'

'Don't worry, my dear,' said the humpback. 'Once our singing starts, it'll spread quickly from whale to whale. Some of us baleen whales can sing to each other across an entire ocean!'

fifty-six

Dulcie spun round in the water, straining to see land or another sea mammal to give them directions. She turned so many times that she lost sense of where the whale was, and cried out in surprise when she saw him.

'So sorry to have startled you,' said the humpback, who had done nothing but stay where he was.

Dulcie had an idea. 'Are you any good at arithmetic? The dolphins I met worked out the shortest route for all the places they had to visit. If they were going to the south coast to find you, and back again, could we work out approximately where the other two places would be?'

'No,' said the whale firmly.

'No,' said Dulcie.

'But if you think they're nearby, I'll send a message to them.' The whale lowered his head and emitted a low moan that turned into a chirrup. He repeated himself several times.

'I'm going to sing in the opposite direction now,' he warned

Dulcie. She moved far away, as his huge body overturned the sea. When the water had settled, the silence seemed deafening. Even the gulls, swooping down for the fish disturbed by the whale, made no cry.

The emptiness was filled with squeaks and squeals. Two silver bodies somersaulted through the air, and plunged again.

Dulcie dived after them. The dolphins circled her, patting her with their flippers and speaking at the same time.

'We've found him at last . . .'

'He wasn't at the coast so we had to calculate the route again!'

'We discovered a new algorithm . . .'

'. . . much faster than the old one.'

'. . . and we haven't lost any time in coming here!'

'But *you* found him too!'

'Thank you all the same,' said Dulcie.

The humpback thrust his snout towards them. 'My dears, could you guide me to the Emerald Isle?'

The dolphins began chattering to him. One of them broke off and turned to Dulcie. 'We'll show him around the coast. What will you do?'

Dulcie remembered the hours she had spent in the sea, alone and directionless. 'Perhaps I could come too? Just to make sure everything goes all right.'

The dolphin smiled. 'And then you must spend the night

with us. I wouldn't like to stay on my own out here. By the way, I'm Eya and this is Kee.'

The humpback offered his fin to Dulcie. 'I'm sure you can swim fast, but I'd feel safer if I knew where you were.'

They set off, the humpback ploughing through the water with Dulcie on his back, the dolphins speeding along beside them. Soon they could hear a constant hissing. Above them, the clouds had opened, releasing rain on to the sea.

fifty-seven

Eager had been introduced to so many people at the exhibition that somehow he never saw the replica mermaid. As they drove back to the Bells' house, he consoled himself with the thought that she would be on display for two weeks. He could visit the exhibition every day if he chose. He immediately felt downcast again. Mrs Bell noticed and said cheerfully, 'Charlotte will be home later. I can't wait to see her. Can you, Eager?'

'No,' said the robot. He hadn't seen the Bells' youngest daughter for nearly a year. Mrs Bell proceeded to tell him how well Charlotte was doing in her medical training. The next thing Eager knew, they had arrived outside the house. He hurried upstairs to Charlotte's room, where he was staying, and lowered his power to process his thoughts.

Halfway through the night, the door opened and Charlotte came in. 'Eager!' she cried in a whisper, throwing her arms around his neck. 'When they announced the Ban was over

I cried. You don't know how much I've missed you over the years.'

'I missed you too,' said Eager.

Charlotte fell on to the bed and kicked off her shoes. 'I've been to a party. I need to sleep. You can stay here.'

'I've rested. I'll go downstairs,' said Eager, getting up from the armchair he'd been sitting in. He found he was clutching Charlotte's teddy bear and propped it against the cushion.

'Have you ever been in love, Charlotte?' he asked.

'Don't talk to me about love,' she said. There was a silence and he realized she had fallen asleep.

fifty-eight

The dolphins led the humpback down the coast. Resting on the whale's back, Dulcie could hear them clicking as they navigated through the night.

After several hours, the high-pitched sounds stopped, and the dolphins faced the whale. 'We're tired, we must rest,' said Kee. 'Now you're through the Strait, you can go on alone.'

'It's very simple,' said Eya. 'When you lose sight of land turn right, and head for the open sea.'

'Once I'm near the Toe, I can call to my friends,' said the whale. 'I am most grateful to you.' He searched the dark water for Dulcie. 'And to you, my dear.' His plump body swam gracefully away.

'I want to rest too,' said Dulcie. She needed to turn down her power and process her thoughts. Like the dolphins, who needed to breathe, she wouldn't switch off completely.

'We have friends here,' said Eya. 'I located their school on the way. It isn't too far to swim back to them.'

There were two dozen or so of the dolphins, most of them already resting on the surface. Dulcie had met numerous different members of the whale family, but never dolphins like these, with their small round heads and marbled bodies.

At dawn she and the bottle-nosed dolphins swam off again. With breakfast in mind, Kee and Eya gave up calculating the shortest possible route in favour of heading straight for the fishing grounds. The moment was near when Dulcie would be alone again. What shall I do now? she thought.

Her only plan had been to contact the whales. There was nowhere she considered home and her sea-mammal friends were constantly on the move. She had last seen them miles away, where she had been captured.

Dulcie said nothing to the dolphins. But as they swam together, Kee nuzzled her hair with her beak. 'Where will you go? You must be with friends, Dulcie.'

The mermaid told her where she had left them. 'The Mediterranean?' exclaimed Eya. 'You should have told us. It's a very long way, and now you're heading in the opposite direction!'

The dolphins began to chatter excitedly and Dulcie found it hard to follow their conversation. Eventually Kee said, 'There are schools of dolphins everywhere en route to the Mediterranean. They'll give you directions.'

'Start with the Grampus dolphins, where we stayed last

night,' said Eya. 'When they've eaten, they can take you out to sea and introduce you to the next school.'

Dulcie flicked her tail. 'That's a good idea,' she said.

Eya said brightly, 'We could calculate the shortest route for you.'

'It won't take long with our new algorithm,' added Kee.

'Thank you,' said Dulcie hastily, 'but I think I should make my own way.'

'As you wish,' said Eya.

The dolphins patted her goodbye. Dulcie watched their sleek bodies skimming the water, until they could no longer be seen. Thanks to them, the whale song would begin. At long last it would encircle the earth and—

She froze. How could she be so stupid? She had been so intent on getting her message to the whales and so excited at finding the humpback that the obvious truth had not dawned on her. The noise in the ocean was not going to stop. For the two robots had betrayed her to Dr Lom and they weren't going to silence the machines.

All this effort for nothing! she thought angrily. Those selfish humans will interrupt the whale song yet again. And the rest of us will suffer!

Why did the robots help her escape in the first place, she wondered. Of course, that was before she had told them her secrets. Perhaps, like LifeCorp, they thought her knowledge was too dangerous to let her go free. Or they had realized her value and made a bargain with Dr Lom. Dulcie slapped the water with her tail. 'Traitors!' she cried. She was tempted to swim back up the river. It would be worth being recaptured to see the two robots again and vent her fury! She checked her foolish thoughts. Going to the city would mean her destruction, and she was determined to survive.

Although she was homeless and betrayed, she wasn't without friends. With a powerful stroke, she headed for the Grampus dolphins to begin her journey south.

fifty-nine

Eager spent the rest of the night in the kitchen, as he used to do when he first lived with the Bells. Later, on his yearly visits, they offered him one of the vacant bedrooms. Sitting in the kitchen again revived old memories. As the house raised the blinds on the morning, Eager realized he hadn't thought about Dulcie at all. The door opened and to his surprise Gavin came in, wearing a dressing gown.

'I decided to spend my last bachelor night in my childhood home,' said Gavin. 'Seeing you here is just like old times.' He reached in the cupboard for a mug. 'I'm making coffee. I feel nervous, though I don't see why I should be. I'm sure I'm doing the right thing.'

'Ask the kettle,' said Eager.

'Not about making coffee,' said Gavin, laughing. 'About marrying Marcia.'

Eager tilted his head. 'How do you know it's the right thing?'

'Well, we miss each other when we're apart,' said Gavin.

'When we met again last summer, I realized I'd been missing her company for years. She felt the same. I'd always thought of Marcia as Fleur's friend. But she's my friend too.'

'And you can be her friend and marry her?' said Eager.

'Oh yes,' said Gavin, smiling. 'It certainly helps to be friends.'

The robot fell quiet. Gavin sat at the table to drink his coffee. 'Are *you* nervous?' he asked Eager.

Eager glanced at him. 'No,' he said, and regretted the half-lie. He wasn't nervous about the wedding, as Gavin thought, but about Sphere and Jonquil stopping the machines in the ocean.

Already it was morning and if Dulcie had succeeded in her plan the whales would begin their singing . . .

'Is something bothering you?' asked Gavin.

For a moment Eager was tempted to confide in his friend. But he remembered Cedric's warning to keep quiet. He didn't want Gavin to pour scorn on Dulcie's mission.

'I'm worried about the rainfall problem,' he said truthfully.

Gavin frowned. 'Yes, you tried to help. Still, the robot think-tank was always a long shot. Perhaps Professor Ogden can shed light on the problem today.'

'Today?' exclaimed Eager. 'Is he coming to the wedding?'

'Marcia invited him. She managed to track him down,' said Gavin. He stood up. 'I'd better hurry and get dressed.'

sixty

Mrs Bell followed her husband down the stairs. They were dressed for the wedding and she stepped carefully in her high heels. 'He needs cheering up,' she said.

'You still haven't explained why he's miserable,' said Mr Bell.

'He's pining for the mermaid,' said his wife.

Mr Bell stopped and looked over his shoulder at her. 'The creature in the tank?'

'The *real* mermaid,' she said. 'I told you – Eager and Cedric released her into the river. LifeCorp would probably have destroyed her otherwise.'

'Well, if she's LifeCorp's property . . .' began Mr Bell.

Mrs Bell sighed. 'Marcia and I thought about this. It isn't clear who she belongs to. Anyway, I'm concerned about Eager. Can't you say something encouraging to him?'

'I'll do my best,' said Mr Bell, carrying on down the stairs.

Eager had laid the kitchen table for breakfast. When Mr and Mrs Bell appeared he told the kettle to make tea and brought a plate of pancakes to the table.

'Thank you, Eager. It feels like a celebration already,' said Mrs Bell. She glanced at the time on her jinn. 'House, you'd better wake up Charlotte.'

A green light by the door flickered.

'Do it gently,' added Mrs Bell.

Mr Bell clapped his hands together. 'How are your sea legs, Eager?'

'I beg your pardon?' said the robot.

'Sea legs,' said Mr Bell. 'You need them to stay upright when your ship rolls. Not that the boat today is likely to roll.'

Eager said, 'Boat?'

'Didn't you know?' said Mrs Bell. 'Gavin and Marcia are getting married at sea. On a floating house of faith.'

The robot stood by the oven, clutching the teapot. After a moment he said, 'When you say floating . . .'

Mr Bell cut him short. 'It's just a regular boat – solar and wind-powered, with fuel as a back-up.'

'Solar power produces electricity, doesn't it?' said Eager.

'It certainly does,' said Mr Bell. 'That's how the kettle boiled the water just now.'

'Talking of which, could we have our tea?' asked Mrs Bell.

The robot moved away from the oven at last and put the teapot on the table. 'If you'll excuse me,' he said, 'I have some thinking to do.'

sixty-one

Eager sat at the bottom of the stairs to think. A sea-going house of faith! If only he had known of Marcia's plans, he would have asked Sphere to include wedding boats along with hospital ships.

He sent a silent message: 'Please, Sphere, don't cut the power to Marcia and Gavin's boat.'

Eager couldn't be sure that Sphere would receive the thought. He imagined Marcia's wrath when the power stopped. As a young girl, she was known for her cross temper. It might be better if he stayed at home. That would be cowardly, he decided. But how could he explain to Marcia what was happening without mentioning Dulcie's mission?

Gavin came downstairs and Eager jumped up to let him pass. He wore a suit with a long, fitted jacket over a tapestry waistcoat.

'Dandy!' called Charlotte, leaning over the mezzanine. She skipped down the stairs after her brother.

Gavin fingered the waistcoat. 'It's a wedding present from Marcia.'

'I'd like to wish you every happiness, Gavin,' said a silky voice. 'Before you leave, I've a poem for you . . .'

Brother and sister exchanged a glance and Charlotte giggled. Eager waited to hear the poem.

'Isn't the flying pod here?' said Gavin but the house was reciting:

'Had I no eyes but ears, my ears would love
That inward beauty and invisible . . .'

Charlotte's mouth fell open. Gavin stood still, beginning to smile as the honeyed voice went on.

Mrs and Mr Bell came into the hallway and listened too.

The house concluded:

'Yet would my love to thee be still as much;
For from the stillitory of thy face excelling
Comes breath perfumed, that breedeth love by smelling.'

Mrs Bell broke into applause. After a second Gavin spoke, in a tone that Eager had never heard before. 'I feel like that about Marcia. Thank you, house. It's the perfect start to my wedding day.'

'We'd better be going,' said Mr Bell.

The front door opened and the family went outside. Gavin was the last to leave. 'House,' he said, 'I don't know how you knew, but you've just said one of my favourite Shakespeare sonnets.'

The house turned on a sensor to follow his progress down the path. 'Shakespeare!' it shrieked. 'Who's Shakespeare?'

sixty-two

Eager sat in the back of the hired hovercar as Mr Bell drove to the river. Ahead of them flew Gavin in the flying pod. When the pod was lost from view, Eager turned his attention to the streets. The temperature was more like summer again and people were strolling, looking carefree.

Mr and Mrs Bell chatted about the friends and relations they would meet at the wedding. Eager was glad to be left in peace. Beside him, Charlotte had reclined her seat and was fast asleep. On his other side, Finbar was looking out of the window.

It won't be long now, thought Eager. He imagined Dulcie and her friends leaping and spinning in the air with joy when the whale song circled the earth once more.

Finbar, too, was busy thinking. He felt happy that his mother was marrying Gavin. All the same, the wedding marked a turning point for him. He would still spend months of the year with his father, but he would no longer go travelling with Marcia. She was putting down roots at last, and he would have to do the same. Marcia and Gavin had talked of buying a house in the city and Finbar hoped they would. He already knew Ju and the Bells, and had begun to make friends at the learning centre. The city was beginning to feel like home.

At the quayside, an animat showed them where to park. A large white vessel floated high above the waterline. Its solar panel wings were tucked back, as if it was a giant swan.

Eager followed the Bells along the gangplank and on to the wide deck. Animats in white uniforms were waiting to serve them drinks. Marcia and Gavin stood in the centre to greet their guests.

Marcia wore a long cream dress with a tapestry bodice that matched the bridegroom's waistcoat. Her chestnut hair, loose about her shoulders, glinted in the sunshine.

'No fuss,' she said, embracing Finbar. 'Just as I promised. We'll say our vows to each other, and people will sing and read poems. Then we'll sail into the afternoon, feasting and dancing.'

Eager dropped his head. If all went to Dulcie's plan, they wouldn't be sailing anywhere.

'It's a long way to the sea,' said Finbar. 'And we can't speed down the river without disturbing other boats – it'll take ages.'

'The captain will explain,' said Marcia airily, indicating a man in a dark blue uniform. She rejoined Gavin to welcome their guests.

The captain grinned at Finbar. 'Since you're interested – the boat is fitted with air cavities that reduce the drag against the water. So we produce less wash. We'll be down the river in no time at all.'

Eager was even more dejected. As long as they remained on the river, the power cut might not affect them. At sea, if the breeze was strong enough, the boat could sail by wind-power alone. But the air was still.

'Dad!' cried Finbar.

Eager turned and saw a man hug Finbar. He had met Amir years before, when he came with Marcia to Fleur and Sam's wedding. But his attention was drawn to the figure behind them. It was Professor Ogden, looking different somehow.

'My face has lost its frown,' said the professor, seeing the robot's puzzled expression. 'I've had my best holiday in years. When I closed my laboratory and said I wanted to go somewhere quiet, Sam suggested I call Amir, who told me about the retreat he visits.'

Finbar overheard him. 'You've been to the mountain! Has it rained yet?'

'Hello, Finbar,' said the professor, shaking his hand. 'I'm afraid it hasn't.' He stepped aside with Eager and lowered his voice. 'I've just been to the compound to see Allegra and Jonquil. They told me of your adventures . . .'

Eager was taken aback. So the professor must know about

Dulcie's plan! Before he could ask, the man winked at him. 'We'll talk later.'

They moved apart as the deck filled with people. The chatter and laughter masked the hum of the engine; it was only when he felt the vibration under his feet that Eager realized they were moving.

The wings had lifted up and the boat glided speedily downriver. 'We'll soon be at sea at this rate,' said a guest. Eager tried to take his mind off the event to come. Around him were half-familiar faces and he concentrated on remembering who they were – relatives and friends of the Bell family, Marcia's parents, her younger brother . . .

Marcia and Gavin had slipped away. Soon Marcia's brother ushered the guests through a doorway decorated with red roses. Eager gazed at the velvet petals and smelt their scent. His mood brightened. Perhaps no one would notice if the boat stopped in the middle of the ceremony.

Inside the house of faith, rows of chairs divided the room into two. At the front was a table, covered with a simple white cloth and bearing a huge display of red and yellow roses.

Eager stopped in his tracks. There were no windows. Hidden ceiling lamps bathed the room in artificial daylight.

'Are you all right, Eager?' asked Sam, who was showing the guests to their seats. The robot didn't reply and Charlotte led him down the aisle to the end of the front row, where

Mr and Mrs Bell, Ju and Fleur were already sitting.

Four musicians in the corner struck up. They wore sculptural white suits and played their instruments remotely, weaving their hands in the air as the sensors sounded the notes. Eager enjoyed the music but he couldn't help glancing at the ceiling lights. If only the ceremony would be over quickly, before they got to sea!

A murmur grew as everyone looked round. Eager swivelled his head to see Gavin and Marcia walking hand in hand towards the table. The tension was too much. When a nearby door opened he jumped up and ran through it, colliding with a small woman in a blue robe. He helped her to her feet. Giving him a backward glance, she hurried into the house of faith.

Eager found himself in a small room. He opened the opposite door and went on to the deck.

sixty-three

Dulcie was having trouble finding the Grampus dolphins. They must have moved a long way from their resting place. Eya and Kee had told her to look out for underwater landmarks: a sheer drop to her right, a large hill, the rotting hull of a ship. She had passed none of these.

A strong current swept against her and she struggled to the surface. The sea was narrowing; there was an island; buildings and boats lined the shore. She was back at the estuary of the river. How ever had that happened?

Dulcie was about to dive when she heard the sound of a speedboat. Her head swung round. The humans were hunting her still. Now she was trapped in the mouth of the river! While she hesitated, a second vessel bore down on her and she veered aside. As the wash of the boat swept her away, she couldn't resist shouting, 'Hey!'

To her surprise, there came an answering call. 'Dulcie!'

The rubbery robot was leaning over the side, waving his

arms at her. She forgot about the speedboat. Her pent up anger burst out. 'Traitor!' she cried, swimming alongside the vessel.

'I beg your pardon?' said Eager.

'Traitor!' repeated Dulcie. 'I trusted you, but you're no better than your human friends! You told Dr Lom I'd escaped. Look – he sent a boat to search for me . . .' As Dulcie looked across at the speedboat, she remembered the danger she was in. But the boat seemed hardly to have moved. She realized she no longer had to swim to keep alongside the larger vessel. Now all she could hear was the lapping of the waves.

'But Dulcie, listen! The engine has stopped!' cried Eager.

Although she was confused – had the robot betrayed her or hadn't he? – she began to share his excitement. But then he gave her a stricken glance and disappeared.

On the deck, Eager faced the rose-covered door. Any moment now, the wedding guests would stumble out into the light. He stepped back to let them pass.

The door remained closed.

Dulcie was calling, 'Well, don't just leave me here! How do I know the humans in the speedboat haven't spotted me?'

He leant over the side again. 'If I could find a ladder, you could climb up.'

'I'm a mermaid, not a monkey,' retorted Dulcie.

'Wait, I can stretch my arms and lift you up,' said Eager,

already unfolding the rubber rings of his legs. He extended his arms over the side and clasped Dulcie around her waist. The sea peeled away as he hoisted her into the air and on to the boat. His limbs contracted to their usual length.

Dulcie looked round at the empty deck. 'What are you doing here?' she asked Eager.

'My friends are getting married in there,' he said, indicating the house of faith.

'Let me see through the porthole,' said Dulcie.

Eager hesitated.

'Hurry up,' said the mermaid, and he carried her over to the door.

'What are these? I like the smell,' said Dulcie.

'Roses,' replied Eager, pleased to share something from his world.

They peered through the porthole. Dulcie saw darkness, lit by tens of tiny stars.

'Candles!' exclaimed Eager.

'Clear the deck!' said a strident voice. 'Clear the deck!'

Tables and benches began to spring up from the floor. Eager kept his back to the wall. Animats climbed out of the hold and began laying the tables.

'Champagne, madam? Sir?' asked an animat-waiter with a tray of drinks.

Dulcie ignored him. 'Eager,' she said, 'listen to the singing!'

A high note, unlike any whale sound she had ever heard, was filling the air.

'It's coming from the house of faith,' said Eager.

The treble voice warbled like a bird before seeming to dissolve into several voices. The animats returned with serving plates of food. They showed no reaction to the singing. Eager cradled Dulcie in his arms as the ululating voice washed over them.

sixty-four

The singing stopped. After a silence the door to the house of faith opened, releasing a swell of excited chatter. Eager scanned the deck in alarm. Short of dropping her back in the sea, there was nowhere to hide Dulcie.

He quickly placed her on the nearest table, scattering glasses and vases of flowers. Animats hurried forward to catch them as Dulcie slapped her tail down. She lay full-length, propping herself on her elbow.

The woman in the blue robe came outside with Gavin and Marcia. 'I never rely on advanced technology,' she was saying, 'nor God, for that matter. Always have matches to hand and a candle under every seat, and buckets of water, just in case.'

'You certainly saved the—' began Marcia. Her jaw dropped when she saw Dulcie as a centrepiece.

Guests spilled on to the deck with exclamations. '*Another* mermaid sculpture! What a wonderful idea!'

'It's a nautical theme!'

'I fancy this mermaid's even more lifelike than the one in your exhibition, Marcia,' said Mr Morris.

A scowl flitted across Dulcie's face.

'Thank you, Dad,' said Marcia stiffly. She and Gavin exchanged a puzzled glance and sat down opposite the mermaid.

'What's going on?' Ju whispered to Finbar. He shook his head.

The captain came on deck to apologize for the power failure. 'We're working hard to fix it. I'm afraid the musicians will have to play their instruments in the traditional way. Luckily the wedding banquet is meant to be cold!'

Although there was a place for Eager at the table, he didn't want to sit there while people ate and Dulcie stared at him. He slipped away into the house of faith. Without the candles it was dark inside. A shadow blocked the light from the doorway, leaving him in blackness.

'I've news for you,' said Professor Ogden. He came to sit beside Eager, and daylight streamed in again. 'Allegra and Jonquil have decided to leave.'

Eager was reminded of Dulcie's words when she had described the technocrats' plan to abandon Earth. 'Not for the moon,' he said, trying to be light-hearted.

'That's precisely where they're going,' said the professor.

The robot gaped at him.

'They're leaving today,' said Professor Ogden. 'On a shuttle that was intended to take the senior technocrats into space.'

'How did you know about that?' asked Eager. 'Did Allegra tell you?'

'Rumours had already reached me,' said the professor quietly. 'But the technocrats can't leave – too many people have discovered their plot. When I told Jonquil that, he said he wanted to go instead. He's been dreaming of a colony of robots, a way to create a world that suits machines like him.'

Eager nodded. This news did not surprise him.

'And why not the moon?' said Professor Ogden. 'Robots don't need air or water, and there are plenty of raw materials up there. There's already a factory to build robots . . .'

'Jonquil will never survive the extreme temperatures!' cried Eager.

The professor gave a chuckle. 'Allegra made him a bubblesuit last night. They're catching the hovertrain to Scotland this afternoon, and I've arranged for a delivery pod to take them to the space centre. While Sam was on holiday he met his former colleagues there. They aren't too pleased that their superiors were planning to leave. Should a robot enter the shuttle and take over the controls, I suspect no one will notice . . .'

Eager took a moment to understand. 'You mean, they'll *pretend* not to notice.' He fell silent. Just as one loss was restored to him, another took its place. Dulcie had reappeared, but his family was leaving. He remembered how Allegra had held his hand when they said goodbye.

'It's a wonderful opportunity for them,' Professor Ogden was saying. 'The International Space Authority has collapsed. There won't be humans on the moon for years. Imagine what they may create in that time!' His tone changed. 'You haven't lost them for good. There's gobetween contact with the moon and one day the shuttles will start again. I wouldn't be surprised if Allegra and Jonquil began to trade with humans . . .'

Eager smiled. The professor's idea was a very human one. 'Allegra could make skis,' he said. The thought of her testing the skis over the lunar surface made him laugh. For a moment his sadness lifted.

Clapping came from the deck and people were calling, 'Speech!'

'I'd better go back,' said Eager.

sixty-five

Gavin smiled broadly at his guests. 'I haven't chosen a best *man*. Instead I've asked someone who's known me since my childhood and been a faithful friend ever since – my best robot, Eager!'

The guests began to clap as Eager came forward. Gavin had asked him to be 'best robot' after the *Robot Einstein* show, but he'd been too busy to think about it. The day before, at the exhibition, he had asked Wag for advice on giving a speech. He had rehearsed Wag's ideas, but seeing Dulcie reminded him of something more important to say. Waiting uneasily for the applause to die down, he looked at Dulcie for encouragement. She glared at him.

Eager had decided to tell the guests not jokes, but truths. He was grateful to humans for building him and he saw many things through their eyes. But the mermaid had set him thinking about the other species in the world. He had always been interested in how humans behaved to each other. Now he realized that it mattered how they treated *all* living things. People seemed to have forgotten that they shared the planet. They were gobbling everything up without a care for tomorrow.

Perhaps if fire had not divided them, humans would remember that animals are their neighbours, thought Eager. He stepped forward to say all this. 'Ladies and gentlemen,' he began.

Every face around the table seemed familiar now. The Bells were looking at him, their eyes shining with affection. Even the Morris family and people he had just met had kindly smiles. He hesitated. 'I want to tell you . . .'

What did he want to tell his friends? How cruel and selfish they were?

'. . . how Marcia and Gavin fell in love. As you know, they were friends for a long time and it was not until Marcia became a professional artist that love blossomed. Gavin watched her paint one day and was overcome with emulsion . . .'

Eager was overcome himself, as the audience chuckled at Wag's joke. He struggled to remember the next line. 'Someone said once, "Marry in haste and repent at leisure".' Eager paused. 'I hope the opposite isn't true.'

The guests took a moment to work this out. They laughed for a long time.

Eager went on, 'Still, you *can* have too much of a good thing. My favourite philosopher, Socrates, died from an overdose of wedlock . . .' He waited for the laughter to die down. 'But here's some good news for you. The machines in the sea have stopped. That's why the lights went out and the boat has no power. I won't tell you how it happened because you won't believe me. Now the whales are singing to each other across the oceans. For once, there are no vibrations to interfere with the song so it will go right around the earth. Water will be healed, and the rainfall will come back to the land.'

He looked at the wedding guests and saw disbelief and amusement, just as he expected. But no one laughed. He decided to try a joke of his own. 'Sea mammals love weddings. They always have a whale of a time. I hope you do too.' He remembered to add, 'So please drink a toast to Gavin and Marcia.'

He sat down hastily to claps and cheers. There were more speeches but he hardly heard them. He was glad he had remembered that it was better to make others happy than sad. And although he could not be sure, he thought he had detected a flicker of approval on Dulcie's face.

sixty-six

After the speeches the guests milled around the deck as the animat-waiters cleared the tables. The musicians began to play jazz.

Professor Ogden led Eager to one side. 'A fine speech,' he said. 'And I believe the water cycle may be back on course . . . Look!' He pointed behind the boat, where clouds were moving gently over the land.

Eager was too nonplussed to be excited about the clouds. 'So you believe what Dulcie said about the whale song?'

'Why not?' asked the professor. 'I'm more humble today than when I was a young scientist. Once I even believed I'd created Sphere, albeit by accident. Now I think it manifested itself. It's a reminder, a guide if you like, to the world behind our surface reality . . .'

'Sphere stopped the noise in the oceans,' said Eager.

The professor nodded. 'At a quantum level Sphere could affect the computers that run the machines.' He frowned. 'But there's a missing link . . . The whale song might well have corrected any imbalances in the water, but why should that restore the rainfall to the land?'

Eager reflected. 'Dulcie said . . .' He stopped. The mermaid must be still on the table, though he couldn't see her through the crowd of guests.

'Yes?' prompted the man.

'She knew the whale song would heal the water. She hoped that would solve the rainfall problem too, but she wasn't sure,' said Eager.

Professor Ogden was staring at the floor of the deck. 'I wonder if it's to do with the krill and the plankton that baleen whales eat . . . ? Yes, that could be it! The tiny plankton release gases into the atmosphere that help clouds to form.'

He began to speak rapidly. 'There are huge quantities of krill and plankton in the ocean and they're constantly on the move. Imagine if they became concentrated in one spot or their movements changed: somehow it might keep clouds linked to the sea. What if the whale song has disturbed the krill and plankton and restored their normal patterns of movement?'

Eager nodded encouragingly.

The professor went on, 'I'm not a marine biologist, and in any case we know so little about the ocean . . . But it's plausible.' He followed Eager's gaze. 'But I can see you have more important things to do, Eager. I'll excuse myself.'

The robot just caught the twinkle in the professor's eye, before leaving him to rescue Dulcie from the table.

sixty-seven

Ju and Finbar were shooing away the waiters who wanted to take Dulcie into the hold. 'They think you're a table decoration,' whispered Ju. 'What are you doing here?'

'I got lost,' hissed Dulcie.

'Lost?' said Finbar. 'I thought you were a reconnaissance agent.'

Eager hurried over to them. 'About time,' said Dulcie.

'What are you going to do with her now?' Ju asked Eager, as if he had *intended* to make Dulcie a centrepiece at the wedding.

'She'll need to be in water soon,' added Finbar.

Eager said helplessly, 'Perhaps there's a bath on board.'

'A bath!' said the mermaid. 'I'll get back in the sea. This boat isn't going anywhere and neither is the speedboat that was chasing me.'

'But then I'll never see you again!' cried Eager, forgetting to keep his voice down.

'Of course you will,' said Dulcie. 'I'll swim up the

river . . .' She broke off, remembering the speedboat. Once its power was restored, it would patrol the river, looking for her. She frowned. 'I can see that you kept your promise to help. But you must have told Dr Lom that I escaped.'

'No,' said Eager hotly. 'He came to the exhibition and—'

Finbar interrupted. 'I hate to spoil a tiff,' he said. 'But if a boat is after you, Dulcie, couldn't it have spotted you at sea? Perhaps the people in it were just curious.'

Dulcie's reply was drowned by shouts and whoops. Several of the guests were leaning over the side of the boat and cheering. 'Porpoises!' called Ju, craning to look.

Ten grey heads were bobbing in the water.

'Don't shout at them, you'll scare them,' said Mrs Morris, coming with the bride to see the cause of the commotion. 'They're not tame ones, are they, Marcia?'

'I didn't arrange this, Mum,' said Marcia, 'any more than I arranged for us to be marooned here.'

Dulcie held out her slender arms to Eager. 'Let me join them,' she whispered.

Her expression was so determined that Eager could see there was no point in arguing. He picked her up again and had barely reached the side when she sprang out of his arms. She dived elegantly into the middle of the porpoises.

The guests cheered again.

Mrs Morris said, 'In all my years as a technocrat, I never saw anything like these mermaids. The tails are so realistic!'

'You've done us proud, Marcia,' said Mr Morris. 'An artist *and* a technocrat!'

Below the surface, the porpoises clustered around Dulcie, talking at once. 'We saw you go on board. We've been waiting for you to leave . . .'

'We hoped you'd come if we dared swim alongside. The seal said you were looking for us . . .'

'He saw you jump in the air! Then the fast boat appeared. He asked us to warn you . . .'

As Dulcie pieced together the information, she realized Finbar had been right. The people in the speedboat must have spotted her when she leapt out of the water on her way to the island.

'Why didn't the seal follow me himself?' she asked.

'You went the wrong way,' said a porpoise, 'and he was scared to go out to sea.'

The mermaid had an unfamiliar feeling. It wasn't a pleasant one. She had forgotten about the jump and had blamed the robot with the kind eyes for betraying her. Now she would have to apologize. But first she needed to know who the people in the speedboat were. 'Thank you,' she said to the porpoises. 'If I can help you one day, I will.'

The porpoises broke into peals of laughter. 'You *have* helped us,' said one. 'You told the whales to sing, didn't you?'

'We just heard it,' said another excitedly. 'We went as far out to sea as we dared. The whole ocean is listening. Come too.'

Watching from the side of the boat, Eager felt his world was crumbling. Once more, Dulcie was swimming away from him, never to be seen again.

sixty-eight

The deck still buzzed with conversation but to Eager the world had gone mute. He leant over the side, watching the speedboat bobbing on the calm sea. Gulls circled noiselessly overhead.

Ju and Finbar stood either side of him. 'Why didn't you tell us about the whale song?' asked Finbar.

'Was it Dulcie's idea?' said Ju.

Eager nodded.

'What exactly is wrong with water?' said Finbar.

Eager repeated what the mermaid had told him. 'It absorbs humans' feelings. When there is too much greed and dissatisfaction the water becomes sick.'

Finbar whistled. 'That's a tough call for humans.'

'Human consciousness is extraordinarily powerful,' said Sam, coming to stand beside Ju. 'Now the Ban is over, research can carry on . . .'

'I know, Dad!' cried Ju, throwing her arms around him.

'And there'll be a scientific revolution! Teleportation, telepathy, telekinesis . . .'

'What's that?' asked Finbar.

'Moving objects at a distance by thought,' said Ju. She waggled her fingers at the speedboat. 'Like this – go boat!'

'You wait and see!' said Sam.

Ju said teasingly, 'Why don't you just ask the whales?'

Everyone laughed, except for Eager. He turned round. 'I don't understand. You're laughing but you don't really find the whale song funny. You all seem to believe me.'

'Why shouldn't we?' asked Ju.

'Cedric said nobody would,' said Eager. 'But Professor Ogden believes me too.'

'Ah,' said Sam. 'Cedric is right, on the whole. The professor and I belong to a dangerous minority of scientists.'

'After the revolution everyone will agree with you,' quipped Ju.

Sam hugged her. 'Exactly. And talking of the power of song . . .'

Amir had joined them at the side of the boat. He was with a young woman in a long gold dress. Sam said to Eager, 'Amir's friend sang one of his poems just now and there wasn't a dry eye in the house of faith.'

'I heard the song from the deck,' said Eager. 'Dulcie and I . . .' He checked himself.

Amir winked at him. 'I know about the mermaid. Finbar told me. It's thanks to her, I imagine, that the whales sang. I've just had a call from my friends at the retreat and it's raining at last.'

'You believe in the whale song too?' exclaimed Eager.

'Why not?' said Amir.

The woman in the gold dress laughed. 'Why should anyone be surprised that whales can heal water?' she asked in her musical voice. 'Have we forgotten why they sing? They're love songs!'

sixty-nine

Dulcie swam past the speedboat gleefully. Without power the people on board could no longer harm her. She was tempted to go closer and listen to their conversation, but the porpoises urged her on. 'It isn't far to hear the whale song,' they said.

Sure enough, the sea soon rang with clicks and chirrups. Dulcie had expected a deeper, richer sound. 'Is that it?' she asked.

'We probably can't hear the low notes because we're not in the ocean,' said a porpoise.

'I still think this is a completely new song,' said one admiringly. 'The patterns are always changing. No other sea mammals sing songs as complicated as these.'

They waited under the surface until they could hear only the echoes of the song. 'Perhaps power is about to return to the machines,' said Dulcie. 'I'd better hurry back to the speedboat.'

The porpoises turned tail and swept her along with them. Dulcie felt the vibration of the engine as she approached. The speedboat was heading towards the river and the floating house of faith. What if the people on board called out to the other vessel? She caught up with them and tuned her hearing to the frequency of humans.

'What do you mean, you think you've spotted her again?' a familiar voice was saying.

The woman Dulcie had heard before said, 'She was at the mouth of the river this afternoon, Dr Lom.'

The doctor's sigh filled the airwaves. 'I've told you already, she's in the city. I had the pleasure of seeing her yesterday afternoon and I can see on the gobetween that she's still there, gracing an art exhibition for the whole world to look at her. And you insist on telling me that you saw her yesterday morning and today!'

'Perhaps it was a different robot . . .' suggested the woman.

'What do you take me for?' exploded Dr Lom. 'Wait, where are you again?'

'The estuary,' said the man's voice.

'That popular area for porpoise-spotting,' said Dr Lom, sounding calmer.

'We haven't seen a single porpoise, I can assure you,' said the woman.

'Would you care to check?' asked the doctor.

Dulcie heard sounds of people scrambling over the deck.

'There are no—' The man broke off.

'I beg your pardon?' said Dr Lom's voice.

'There *are* porpoises now,' said the man. 'In fact, we seem to be surrounded by them . . .'

'Leaping out of the water!' cried the woman. 'Seven, eight, nine . . .'

'Well, there is your jumping mermaid,' said Dr Lom. 'So you'd better return to shore.'

The porpoises seemed to have forgotten their shyness as they dipped in and out of the water alongside the speedboat. Dulcie called goodbye and swam towards the house of faith. Loud music was coming from the deck. She was surprised to see Eager leaning over the side again.

'Dulcie!' he cried, stretching out his arms to haul her aboard.

'What do you want me to do?' said Dulcie. 'Sit on the wedding cake? I'm staying in the sea, where I belong.'

'Then why have you come back?' asked Eager.

The mermaid stared at him and looked away. At last she held his gaze. 'I've come to apologize.'

'Pardon?' said Eager, who hadn't heard her clearly.

'Apologize,' shouted Dulcie. 'I thought you had told Dr Lom I'd escaped down the river. I was wrong. I'm very sorry. You helped me and I didn't trust you. I'm very sorry indeed.'

'It's all right, Dulcie,' said Eager. 'I accept your apology.' He felt a hand on his back.

'Eager,' said Charlotte gently. 'Be bold.'

He looked over his shoulder at her. 'Bold?'

Charlotte nodded.

Eager went back to the mermaid. 'Listen, Dulcie. I will be at the river tomorrow afternoon. Remember where Cedric carried you? Come there. I shall wait for you.'

Her emerald eyes flashed. He couldn't tell whether she nodded or not. With a toss of her tousled hair, she was gone.

epilogue

Marcia came to the door to greet the reporter. He looked past her into the sitting-room with its view of the river. His eyes lit up. 'I see your family is here.'

'My husband and my son,' said Marcia. 'And this is my niece.'

Ju waved at him from her floor cushion.

'A family picture would be wonderful,' said the reporter.

'No,' said Marcia tartly. 'You're here to discuss my work.'

The man sighed as she led him to a chair by the window. He tried a different tack. 'I noticed one of your trademark mermaids as I walked along the river.'

'I can't take all the credit for them,' said Marcia, flashing a smile. 'Anyway, that was last year. Now, about my return to making pots . . .'

Half an hour later the reporter left. Marcia threw herself on to the sofa beside Gavin. 'Why do they always ask about the mermaids?'

Gavin put his arm around her. 'They'll soon forget about them. Meanwhile, it's the perfect way to protect Dulcie. Whoever built her knows that she's here. It should be clear by now that she isn't going to reveal any secrets. In any case, her knowledge is out of date. There's no point in kidnapping her, quite apart from the international outcry it would cause.'

Finbar said, 'I can see the headline: *Living sculpture stolen from world's favourite artist!*'

Marcia threw a cushion at him.

'How long is Dulcie staying this time?' asked Ju.

'We've no idea,' said Gavin. 'She comes and goes.'

'We were so lucky to find this house,' said Marcia. 'If our wedding boat hadn't been stranded I'd never have seen the porpoises and decided I must live near them.'

Finbar nodded in agreement. He loved the house and the trip by riverboat to the learning centre in the city.

'Where exactly do the porpoises live?' asked Ju.

Marcia pointed out of the window. 'Further down in the estuary, but they often swim up here.'

Ju said, 'Is Dulcie friends with them?'

'Oh yes,' said Marcia.

'I think she finds them a bit boring, though,' said Finbar. 'She spends most of her time near the house, by the jetty.'

'Really?' said Ju, raising her eyebrows.

'Really,' said Finbar, grinning.

* * *

Eager sat on the jetty, watching a dragonfly hover on the water. Life was good. He helped Gavin and Marcia in the house or went with Finbar to the learning centre. Soon Cedric and Olga were coming to stay and Finbar was taking the robots to see Wag's new show. And every day Eager could walk in the woods near the river and meet Dulcie . . .

'It's time I joined the dolphins again,' she said. 'I miss the open sea.'

Eager's system somersaulted. 'I understand. You're at home in the sea.'

'Is that all you can say?' asked Dulcie.

Eager noticed the dragonfly fly off. 'I shall miss you,' he said.

'Will you?' said Dulcie. She flipped on to her back, the trace of a smile on her lips.

'When are you leaving?' asked Eager.

'Oh . . . in a while,' said the mermaid, closing her eyes.